STEVEN SPARROW

- & -

the Shade of a Great Tree

BOOKS BY MATTHEW DALE JONES

The Cup Makers Guild

Steven Sparrow & the Shade of a Great Tree

STEVEN SPARROW

- & -

the Shade of a Great Tree

a novel by

Matthew Dale Jones

ISBN-13: 978-1-7354948-2-1

For Curtis Dale Jones,

the first writer I knew

CONTENTS

Part Three – The Great Tree

PART ONE

The Nest

CHAPTER ONE

While We Take to the Sky

"THE RIVER ROARED, the frothy, blue water surging, urging to be reunited with its Mother Ocean. The sun sizzled overhead, as once rough rocks succumbed to the river's persistent force, their smooth, slick exteriors a beautiful reminder of Nature's power to change the seemingly unchangeable. The river would not be denied." Steven paused for suspense. "The mighty, muscular salmon, however, had other plans."

The flock shuddered. Hushed gasps and murmured questions floated amongst the dancing green leaves. The sparrows gathered on nearby branches were spellbound.

Steven stood stock still on the outer rim of his family's Nest, his pudgy, fuzzy feathered body radiating the confidence of an orator with an enraptured audience eating from his wing. He waited for the tension to become unbearable.

"What were their plans?" a voice from the crowd urgently called out.

"What is a salmon?" chirped a young voice.

Steven was delighted, choosing to hold the pause a moment more.

Brother, meanwhile, was fuming. He and Sister were stuck cleaning the Nest, *again*, while Steven regaled a crowd with a stupid story. Nobody understood half the frilly nonsense that poured out of his beak (he suspected that Steven didn't either), but they sure lapped it up. Even Mother fell victim to Steven's verbal gas, getting tricked into smelling the flowers he was describing instead of the putrid fart he was covering up.

The smile on her face while she prepared breakfast let Brother know she was listening to Steven, inhaling the daffodils again.

Father crashed through the outer leaves and landed on a branch above, returning from his last-minute preparations for Flying Day. He paused to take in the scene before hopping down to their Nest.

"About time," Brother mumbled to himself, knowing Father was less tolerant of Steven's talent for skipping out on chores.

"Steven, come here, please," Father commanded, firmly yet gently, the gathered eyes calming the tone he would have preferred to use.

"Forgive me friends, but I am needed elsewhere. We shall learn the fate of the salmon when we reconvene. Will they make it upstream? Will the river thwart their mission? And what about—the Grizzly King?" Steven held the moment, his eyes wide to increase the drama. Many in the crowd placed their wings on each other to keep themselves from falling off their branch. All breathing paused. "We shall learn of their fate next time. Until then, farewell." The flock blurted their groans of displeasure at having to wait, but then quickly recovered with enthusiastic hoots of appreciation. Steven bowed and joined his family in the Nest as the crowd dispersed.

"Help your brother and sister," Father said distractedly, his mind back on the day ahead.

Steven opened his beak, a stinky gasser ready to escape.

"Breakfast is ready!" Mother sang to prevent an argument from starting. "Let's make sure we fill up. Big day today!"

Flying Day was not a *big* day, it was the *biggest* day of the year. The entire sparrow community buzzed with excitement as fledglings left the Nest and learned how to activate one of the greatest gifts in the Kingdom of Creatures. Everyone got a good glimpse at the adult birds they were becoming as every imaginable way of exiting the Nest and becoming a flyer—from gleeful and manic to scared and timid and everything in between—could be witnessed on Flying Day. It's been said that a line drawn between Flying Day and any other day in a sparrow's life would make sense.

The parent teachers ran the gamut too. Warm demanders that gave clear and concise instructions to meet their reachable expectations. Nervous wrecks that would rather their children just sat in the safety of their Nest and watched while they did all the flying for them. Pushovers that always said "yes" and thought everything their kids did was brilliant. Highly strung perfectionists that were impossible to please.

In the end, every young sparrow found their way into the sky because it was the Way. Leaving the Nest was how they learned, how a young sparrow took ownership of their life, and when their parents knew it was time to let go. It wasn't easy for anyone, but it wasn't supposed to be. Life was hard for sparrows, and they needed to be ready for a world that could be brutal and impatient.

Father had fond memories of his own Flying Day. He had become one of the strongest flyers in their community, and others respected him because of it. Mother didn't like to admit it—she thought it made her look shallow— but seeing him fly that first time was what set her heart fluttering and convinced her he was the one for her.

Father had been looking forward to this day ever since his children had broken free from their shells. He knew all three of his children were going to need very different methods of instruction. He was prepared with tactics and strategies that would be effective for each of their personalities.

Mother had been looking forward to the day as well. The thought of watching her husband coach their children was enough to get tears welling up. Sometimes at dinner she would start crying for reasons only known to her. The Nest would fall silent until she relieved the tension with a warm smile. She'd say, "I'm just so happy," as she looked at all of them and they returned to eating.

One thing Mother and Father had not anticipated, however, was Steven's response to being told that lessons were going to begin after breakfast.

"I believe that I shall walk, for flying's not my bag," Steven told them. *Not my bag* was the kind of stuff that flowed out of him.

Once Steven put something on the record, it was one hundred and twelve percent true. This declaration, however, was not a harmless tall tale or an attempt to skip out on some chores; this was a defiant statement in opposition to fundamental bird stuff, like a fish choosing not to swim. Even Steven—who clearly did not grasp the gravity of his choice—was a little startled he made the decision so rashly, so flippantly, but he made it, and there was no chance he was reversing direction.

Father was a strong, proud sparrow. Steven's announcement had left him dressed in a tight jumpsuit of embarrassment. It was starting to cut off his circulation.

He chuckled nervously while Mother stayed silent. She knew how her son was once he said something, and she knew that in his young life nothing had ever been taken back. In fact, things only became more so (that's where the extra twelve percent came in). Mother knew who her children were. Father knew who they could be. It's what made them such a good team.

Father believed he still had influence, that things could be changed. These were foolish beliefs, but the graveness of the situation invited foolishness. Mother, however, was one hundred and twelve percent convinced Father would be blowing his top before too long.

She knew Father's actions in the moments to come would not be effective. She also knew there were no actions he could take that would produce the outcome he was seeking. She let Father be, affording him the space given to those we love. She knew he would never go too far, and he needed to do everything he could in the ways he knew how. Her heart both swelled and ached.

"But son, birds fly! That's just what we do!"

Father couldn't believe he had to say this. He had said it louder than intended, and with an air of authority he felt was necessary to dislodge Steven from this silly joke. Surely it was a joke, right? A lousy one if you asked Father.

C'mon now! It was Flying Day for crying out loud! One of the most glorious days in any bird's life, where they leave the Nest for the first time and tumble through the sky, awkwardly learning how to move their wings just so to harness the winds, the thrill of a thousand roller coaster rides compounded into a single, unforgettable moment. In his peripheral vision, Father could see flashes of erratic flight paths as children were taking to the air. His Nest was in a holding pattern.

Steven was quiet, which surprised everyone. He was approaching one hundred and four percent. Father continued.

"There's nothing quite like flying through the sky and all that blue!"

Father was becoming desperate, throwing his wings skyward, almost screaming. His voice was hoarse and blustery like the gusty winds that had begun to knock leaves from the bushes. Getting away without doing some chores was one thing, but choosing not to fly? Who does that? What would the other parents think? This thought, that other parents would be judging Father's inability to get his child to fly, started a fire in his chest that would soon burn a hole straight through.

Had a father bird ever had to persuade their child like this? Father admitted the answer may be "yes," especially considering many believed young birds should be classified as a different species until they matured. He was certain no parent had ever had a child follow through with their threat. It was unimaginable to Father that any creature could possess such a gift and ignore it.

Steven was unaffected by the frustration growing in his father. He was at one hundred and seven percent and climbing.

This was clearly not a joke. Father was not going to convince Steven, and the Way was the Way. Flying Day may need to be renamed Leaving Day, a distinction Father was not thrilled to be associated with.

Before the fire inside consumed him and he did or said something he regretted, Father lifted from the Nest. The angry force of his flapping wings caused all those nearby to duck their heads. He crashed through a few twiggy limbs, banked left, and was out of sight before anyone turned their eyes skyward to see where he had gone. Mother knew he wouldn't be landing anywhere until he'd worked out some things in his head. He did his best thinking in the air, alone.

Mother was silent. The look on her face gave no indication of the turmoil gathering inside of her. Defiance was hardening inside Steven, like cement that soon wouldn't accept your scribblings. It was fueled by his unfailing belief he was right. This default setting is not uncommon in young birds, but Steven suffered from an aggressive form of the affliction. Mother knew children were not the only ones that suffered from this disease. Only her blank, emotionless stare slowed Steven's progress. He stalled at one hundred and seven percent.

"What do you think, Mother, about your son, the walking bird?"

Mother's silence was unsettling to Steven.

"I love you," she said after a long spell, failing to make eye contact. She turned and flew away to process how she felt. Like most mothers, she was rarely alone, but this moment required solitude. She needed more than she was ever going to be afforded. The pain was more severe than she had the capacity to grasp. It caught her off guard. She had no point of reference, and the confusion amplified into something that left her feeling lost.

This left Steven and his two siblings alone in the Nest. Needing to regain higher ground, Steven turned to them to justify his decision.

"Mother and Father would have me feel like I am something less than a full sparrow for making a personal decision I have the right to make! Any sparrow can fly, but has there ever been one that has *chosen* to walk? The answer is NO! Until me, that is. And guess who else chooses to walk? Humans! Ever heard of them? Only the most dominant animal on the planet! What about bears? Walk! Wolves? Walk! So, I, Steven Sparrow, am choosing to walk like the greatest of beasts, and our parents want to shame *me*? Well, shame on *them*!"

The mercury began to rise again as Steven was impressed with his impromptu argument. He was working to gain his own favor as much as his siblings'. It worked. One hundred and nine percent.

Sister was a peacemaker. Her mind was racing like a hummingbird to think of the right thing to say that would restore the calm and stability that had been life in their Nest to this point. Conflict made her nervous.

"Just give them some time, Steven. They'll come around. Your idea is so new, so unique, like most of the things that fly out of your mouth." *Oh my, did I just say that?* She paused right after her unfortunate phrasing, glancing at Steven with a look of apology.

Seeing that Steven was dealing with his own swirling thoughts, she realized the phrase flew right over his head. *Oh, jeez, I did it again!* Sister thought to herself before realizing that the second misstep was just an internal, non-vocalized thought. She hurried to continue before her nerves got the best of her. "Mom and Dad are very traditional, you know that, but they love you. Just give it some time." *Phew!*

She put her wing around him and worked hard to squelch the thoughts ping-ponging around in her head from coming out her beak, let alone revealing themselves on her face. She buried her face in his feathers to obscure any uncontrolled ticks.

We are BIRDS! she wanted to scream.

We're made of feathers and wings!

Stop being so stubborn and stupid, you…you…you ding-a-ling!

Instead, she just hugged him, hoping heated heads would cool.

Brother, on the other wing, was not as tactful when it came to expressing himself. Steven's skillset had earned him the lion's share of attention, but Brother knew he was going to kick Steven's butt in the air. While Steven had exercised his beak, Brother had readied his body. Even Brother knew you didn't fly with your beak. He had been looking forward to this since birth, and he was annoyed that Steven had found a way to make Flying Day all about him. It was time to start kicking butt.

"I believe our Nest has been infested with a Dodo bird! Go ahead and walk, you fool, while we take to the sky!"

Brother fell silent as Steven turned and looked at him, fierce, angry pools of tears collecting in his eyes. Steven squinted to hold back the flood, mustering all the stubbornness he had left. He didn't have any. Tears and snot began to flow.

One hundred and twelve percent.

CHAPTER TWO

This Impulse of the Heart

MOTHER WAS ALONE on a high branch in the Great Tree, the tallest and largest tree in the territory. Its trunk was as round as fifty trees, and its mighty limbs thicker than fat pigs. Each limb reached to claim its own acreage of sky. The overlapping canopies they produced cast mottled shade throughout the day as the sun traced its arc. There wasn't a spot of land in this corner of the world not at some point in the day or year made cooler by the Great Tree.

Mother was thinking about Steven. Could this be the moment he changed, where the words were expressed only to amuse or evoke a reaction but not to trigger the behavior that followed? Would he reflect on the error of his choice and make a correction? Could he be persuaded to change after witnessing the agony he was causing others? She knew an apology was out of the question. The river of excuses would be tolerable and expected, but was she hoping for too much?

She knew she was, and the sadness that settled in was making her lightheaded. She knew one day Steven's unbendable will—a powerful tool that could be wielded towards greatness—would reveal its limits the natural way, through experiencing the pain of its misguided application. She just didn't think it would come so soon or with such an important matter. Choosing not to breathe was the only decision she could see as being worse.

Swelling inside her was a desire to wrap her son up in her wings and insist he stay in the Nest. She was desperately trying to convince herself this was a temporary phase, her son was a late bloomer, seeing his siblings and other young sparrows fly would inspire him to do the same. But this impulse of the heart was not something she could act upon. She knew leaving the Nest was the Way.

Her Steven would just need to leave by talons instead of wings. Grief grabbed her heart and began to squeeze so hard her limbs tingled from lack of blood. The image of her son alone on the ground began to compress her lungs. All that was alive in her, all the blood and oxygen was being squeezed out like paint from a tube. Thoughts of her other children kept it from being a feeling she welcomed.

Father landed on her branch. He was out of breath from the non-stop hard flying he'd been doing. His head was clearer now, but the darkness seizing his wife seeped into him. He wished there was something he could do to absorb all of it and set her free. Saving her became his priority. She was always his priority, and the reminder was comforting.

"We must let him go, my dear. It's how all creatures learn. It is the Way."

His voice wavered as he said it. He was only saying aloud what they knew to be the truth. They sat in silence, the tips of their wings touching. They waited for the hurt to evaporate and allow them to return to the Nest. Like used towels tossed into a closet and forgotten, their hearts were crumpled and damp with sorrow.

CHAPTER THREE

The Weight of His Predicament

"I'LL SHOW YOU! I'll show you all!" squelched Steven through the tears, his chest puffed out to mask the overwhelming dread that soaked him. Dread, especially the overwhelming variety, could stop most creatures in their tracks, but Steven was operating at one hundred and twelve percent. Action won out.

Caught in the swift moving riptide of his will, he was being swept towards an uncharted ocean. Instead of clawing his way back, he was paddling with it, zooming to nowhere as fast as he could. Steven had never faced opposition like he had this morning from his family. There was no way, absolutely *no way* he was going to fight against his rabid urge to prove them wrong.

Luckily for Steven, their Nest was in a small dogwood that was more bush than tree, giving him a complex web of limbs and leaves to grab onto as he made his way out of the Nest and to the ground. A few times on his journey down, the web broke his short fall. One time it left him dangling upside down, his legs hooking onto a branch as he plummeted headfirst towards the ground after a misstep. But Steven never looked back to see if Brother or Sister noticed.

The bush was dense. The blustery winds caused the limbs and leaves to rub up against each other, making the wonderful music only Mother Nature could orchestrate. Brother and Sister swore they heard a subtle sobbing sound distinct from all others. It created a somber symphony that would haunt them for longer than they knew.

For hours Steven rushed aimlessly through the underbrush, his only goal to get as far away as possible. Instincts steered him from open areas. His eyes were locked in the forward position. *Go, go, go* his heart raced.

Crack! Crash! Thud! Steven dove into a clump of tall, thick grass, not knowing what was coming after him. He laid shaking, his beak pushing into the earth as he tried to make himself flat, willing himself to become one with the ground. He imagined he was a heavy boulder, its weight pressing down from above, gravity's hand pulling with equal force from beneath, sinking, sinking, sinking, until nothing of Steven could be seen above ground. Despite his attempt to manifest otherwise, only his forehead and belly touched the ground. He could taste the crumbling earth as it pushed through the crack of his beak. Luckily for Steven, the clump of grass hid his squishy and very much above ground body.

Nothing came towards him. He plucked his beak out of the ground and craned his neck to peer in the direction of the noise. There on the ground was a young sparrow that he recognized. She lived in a nearby nest and had attended some of his stories. They had never spoken to each other, but Steven had noticed her in a way he hadn't noticed most others. Something about how she held herself made Steven think she would be comfortable and easy to be around. He had an impulse to call out to her, but he didn't.

She got herself up, and Steven could see frustration and fear pushing down on her like the boulder he wished had smushed him into the earth.

Some dirt trickled down to the back of his throat and he gagged. He pushed his face into the ground to muffle the noise.

Her head turned towards the clump of grass, and she froze.

The air fluttered overhead and limbs creaked as two adults landed in a small tree halfway between where Steven lay and the crash-landed sparrow stood, stooped and weary. She broke her gaze away from the grass and looked up at the new arrivals.

"Are you okay?" one of the adults asked.

"Yeah, not bad. Not as painful as the last one." She sighed a defeated sigh. "I still can't get it, Dad. I suck at this."

"You're doing really good. You're actually picking this up faster than I did."

The young sparrow scrunched her face and looked at the other adult. "Is that true, Mom?"

Mom produced a gentle smile and nodded her head. "Your Dad was a slow learner, if I remember correctly. Like, really slow. Really, really, really slow. But he kept at it, and look at him now. He only crashes once a week. It used to be every day."

"Hey now, enough of the dad bashing." They all shared a laugh.

The fear and frustration that had been pushing down on the young sparrow's shoulders fell off. She stood up straight and bounced a couple times, moving her head around. She looked fresh and ready.

The young sparrow brushed herself off and launched into the air while the two adults watched from their perches.

Their eyes were glued to the sky.

"Did you hear about that boy Steven, the one that tells all those stories," Mom said.

"No, what?" replied Dad as their heads followed their child's path.

"I'll fill you in tonight. We should go join her. Just know I don't envy his parents. They have their hands full. We're pretty lucky with her." They gave each other a knowing glance and then rocketed into the sky, together.

Steven sped off, moving faster than he had all day.

As night descended, making the dark area even darker, Steven continued to stumble forward. On occasion, his talons sank into muddy mush or caught on a tangle of exposed roots, and cowardice warned *Go back!*

NOOOO! he screamed in response. The voices in his mind were locked in a battle of wills.

The emotional and physical distress took its toll. Exhaustion and fear tensed his every feather and made it nearly impossible to continue. He had never been so scared in his life, nor as tired, but turning back was not an option. Nobody would get the satisfaction of seeing Steven Sparrow admit defeat. *Nobody!*

Steven did not know why he said what he said. When the pain and fear allowed room for pondering, he tried to settle on a reason.

Am I afraid of heights?

Am I worried that I won't be as good as Brother and Sister?

Am I afraid I'll let Father down?

It didn't matter. He had decided. He was going to be Steven Sparrow, the one who did what no other sparrow had done. Stubbornness was not a bad thing, he thought. He was no different than Father when it came to being inflexible. They saw themselves as determined, not stubborn. He was *determined* to live by his rules only. If it didn't start in his head, no thank you.

The deeper these thoughts sank in, the more he came to love them. To him that night, high on anger and fatigue, Steven the Walking Sparrow sounded legendary.

His young legs could carry him no further. He collapsed to the ground beneath a dense bush. Not a speck of moonlight made its way to the ground. Dead leaves blanketed the cool, moist dirt. Steven scooped them up and made a pile upon himself. Just another random clump of leaves, no small, exhausted birds to see here, no siree. He knew how vulnerable he was. Creatures would be lurking in the dark, creatures that liked to eat tired, defenseless birds that took to sleeping on the ground, instead of in trees where they were safer.

He had no energy to move, and he hoped his pile was enough to keep him alive. His eyes grew heavier than they'd ever been. Dreams of his family in the Nest danced in his head, bathing Steven in a soothing, druggy medicine, easing the pain and sending him into the deepest slumber of his life.

No sooner had his eyes closed when he felt the sun's rays begin to warm the air, sanding down the prickly cool of night. His eyes, crusted shut from tears and soil, took great effort to open. Once they did, all he saw was a fierce amber glow as the sun drilled into the leaves from its low position in the sky. With his brain no longer clouded, the weight of his predicament came crushing down, as if he were buried beneath stones instead of leaves. He was a bird, a walking sparrow, and he was alone. He had rejected the sky.

There was movement nearby, as leaves began to rustle in the still morning air. Somebody was moving towards him! *Did Father organize a search party?* (He would never admit it, but that thought filled him with joy and cast off the stones he'd just been crushed by. He would feign resistance, of course, but he wanted nothing more at that moment than to be with his family.)

What he heard was not a party, and it wasn't a bird. It was a single creature. He couldn't make out what it was. Steven had not moved, so his hiding place beneath a pile of leaves was intact. There were fanged monsters that could see through attempts at diversion, using senses other than sight to locate the unseeable. He prayed this was not one of them.

There was nothing he could do to escape; his body was still wracked with pain. Any movement seemed an impossible request of his body. All he could do was close his eyes and hope the killer would be quick, one crushing blow to snap his hollow bones like feeble sticks.

"What are you doing here?" a voice squeaked, its high pitch slicing through the air. "There's a vicious cat that prowls these parts. Come quick! Let's disappear!"

A small paw reached into the pile and grabbed at his right wing and tugged, prompting Steven to hurriedly get up. His muscles screamed their disapproval. Leaves slid away as he followed the tugging paw, blinded by the sun flooding into the area where he had slept.

Sightlessly he went along before descending into a hole in the ground. The entry was a tight squeeze, curves in the path causing him to bonk his head on the wall multiple times before correcting to the new direction. He learned the design was purposeful, its inconveniences built to persuade probing paws to search elsewhere.

Once inside the dwelling's only room, Steven's eyes adjusted to the light that trickled in. Shiny bits and bobs were placed here and there to lure it underground. The room was swept clean, and outside of a few gathered clumps of raw cotton that bore the dampened outline of a resting rodent, the room was barren. After taking in his surroundings, his eyes settled on his host.

Before him was a mouse, made from taut, gray wires humming with nervousness, his eyes two small, black seeds. His round ears twitched forward and back, confused—attentive or passive? He was skinnier than Steven believed a mouse should be. He exuded a brittle strength, a strength born in the Great Attack. That's what Mouse called it, the day Cat came upon his prior home, where he lived with his parents and siblings, the family Cat made sure he'd never see again.

"What is wrong with you? A bird sleeping on the ground?" Mouse chastised. His face was fixed with disbelief. "You have wings to soar from evil beasts that like to hunt for creatures like us!"

Mouse, having gone through what he'd gone through, could not fathom such a choice. If only he and his family had been able to fly away.

Where Steven talked elegantly to entertain, to get attention and praise, and sometimes to obscure the truth, Mouse's words came out in nervous streams, with minimal punctuation, and were never more than a millimeter from the truth. At least as Mouse understood things. Steven was still adjusting to the bewildering turn his life had just taken, causing the door between his brain and beak to be temporarily locked. Mouse filled the pause with a detailed account of the Great Attack.

Mouse believed in getting things out in the open, full disclosure, transparency, that kind of stuff, but it didn't mean he wasn't also a good listener. In fact, he was a great listener. When he fixed his beady black eyes on you, his whiskers like antennae, bending your direction to receive the communication not sent in soundwaves, you knew it was your turn to talk, and you had his full attention. That's the pose he struck once he was done sharing.

Steven was now able to talk because all the thoughts and ideas his brain produced while "listening" to Mouse had piled up behind the locked door and overwhelmed it, breaking it from its hinges (his brain worked like a movie theater's popcorn machine with a never-ending supply of kernels, pop, pop, popping away, spilling over the edge before pushing out the door to begin overwhelming the lobby and anyone gathered there).

He went on and on about how ridiculous his parents were being, the callousness of his brother—Sister was spared criticism—about the injustice of the expectation that he fly just because he was a sparrow, about the benefits of walking over flying, about the heroic nature of his quest to open up new opportunities for future sparrows, and other convincing arguments that made him lying under a pile of moist leaves, alone in the dark to seem logical, progressive even. It was, without a shadow of a doubt, brave, even if Steven did say so himself, which he did. Multiple times.

When he was done, Mouse reversed his thoughts about flying, was grateful to be earth-bound like Steven, and apologized for his earlier outburst.

"Apology accepted," said Steven.

Steven prophesied their new relationship was a matter of fate, that these two orphans—he would often bend words to mean what he wanted them to mean—were brought together for a purpose of some magnitude, one Steven would be able to describe in more detail once he'd gotten better sleep, and maybe some food. For now, they agreed to soldier on together, to continue as brothers of choice, the best kind there were, according to Steven.

Mouse, who'd had a traditional kind of brother, wasn't in a place to argue with Steven because he had never had this other kind of brother, the choice kind. He also didn't want to upset his new friend, so he decided to keep his opinions about the best type of brother to himself. *Why does there need to be a best kind?* The idea puzzled him. He eventually settled on just appreciating the one he had.

He was just so happy to no longer be alone.

PART TWO

The Zoo

CHAPTER FOUR

When One Must Suffer

MOUSE WAS COURSING with joy so electrifying the temperature in their home jumped several degrees warmer in minutes. To partner with a bird! He could not believe his luck, but his inborn nervousness, coupled with the Great Attack trauma, instilled a hypersensitive cautiousness that kept any gaskets from being blown.

Steven, too, was energized by his good fortune to find a friend so quickly after leaving home. Steven, being who he was, reasoned luck played no part in his new situation, but it was the only possible outcome given his enormous talents (he was skilled at ignoring details that poked holes in his theories). The great question nagging Steven was why more hands hadn't reached into the leaf pile, tugging him every which way towards an endless number of homes and partnerships.

The only possible answer was Mouse must have been the fastest of the bunch, and the temporary blindness Steven experienced at extraction must have obscured all the other creatures and their forlorn expressions at losing out on such a prize. Yes, that must be it. Since this was the only possible answer, he did not need to interview Mouse for corroboration. Case solved and filed away.

The energy in the spartan room subsided, and gurgling sounds were heard, as if the upstairs neighbor had flushed the toilet. Mouse had no indoor plumbing or upstairs neighbor, so their tummies were eventually identified as the source. They were famished, their excitement waning enough for them to be reminded through gastric blurts and gyrations.

Mouse was embarrassed he had no food to offer his new roommate. He limited his excursions to the bare minimum, but now that he had a partner to venture out with, he felt more emboldened.

"I know a place where seeds fall from the sky!" Mouse exclaimed, proud to share his knowledge. He suggested they hurry out, collect as much as they can, hurry back, have a delicious meal, and enjoy the slumber of a lifetime considering how exhausted they each were from the incredible day they were having.

Several times he emphasized the importance of sticking to the tall grass, even if it took longer to get where they were going. Mouse used no punctuation and very few spaces. Steven was not a practiced listener, so he only caught thirty-six percent of what Mouse said.

Mouse led them out and scurried to the lead, as he knew where the seeds fell. Steven hopped closely behind. The promise of food amplified Steven's hunger, and the mild gurgles turned into strangled squawks, sounding like a baby pterodactyl screaming at his mother to drop a prehistoric rodent into its long, snapping beak.

These were the kinds of images produced without notice in Steven's head. As it took shape and played like a cartoon in his mind, he remembered how he would turn such moments into entertaining tales at the Nest. He wanted to see if Mouse would respond with similar enthusiasm, but what he got instead was a stern shushing when he opened his beak. Mouse was a focused fellow, Steven thought, incapable of multi-tasking. Oh well, his loss.

Steven was also observing that he was more of a *hopper* than a *walker*, wishing he could go back to that moment with his mother and re-state a more accurate description of his intended mode of transportation. Maybe it would have produced a different response. Maybe Mother would not have flown away.

This last thought left him abruptly as he found himself submerged in murky water, flailing around at the bank of a pond like an animal trying to demonstrate the full range of motion their unique body was capable of. It was as if he was modeling for Leonardo DaVinci—Steven as *Vitruvian Sparrow.*

He found himself there after tripping over a broken branch and stumbling forward before slipping on a mossy stone and doing a half flip backwards. The flailing stopped when he realized he needed only to stand up. Steven came to the sobering conclusion that pondering and walking, or more accurately pondering and hopping, were not activities he should engage in simultaneously while tramping through new territory.

"Oh, my dear! What have you done?" Mouse sputtered in a screamy whisper. His internal alert system was blaring at a level reserved for incoming nuclear missiles. "Reach out and take my hand." Again, Mouse tugged Steven to safety, and again, no immediate "thank you" was heard. For someone so naturally gifted with communication, the simplest and most important phrases escaped Steven.

A bassy, velvety "RIBBIT!" startled them, and the jigglier parts of Steven danced to the sonic force of the exclamation. For Steven, it felt like he was standing next to a large subwoofer. The pulsing waves became visible as they travelled through his less than firm torso. The sensation was delightful. The wonderful tickle worked its way through, and he giggled uncontrollably.

"Shhh! We must be quiet!" warned Mouse, his beady eyes full of worry and ink.

"Hey boys, you caught me by surprise!" croaked Frog as he vaulted from the bog, his bulbous body landing inches from Steven and Mouse. Frog's large smile extended beyond the circumference of his face, and Steven sensed that if he were to have a tail, it would be wagging enthusiastically. He was here to play fetch, not attack.

Steven's beak fell open, agape in astonishment at the sight of this new creature, so fleshy, soft, and green. He began his assessment of this friendly creature.

Frog was a fellow hopper, but his plodding method was off-putting and painful to observe. His oddly shaped body did not have any design advantages Steven could discern. Steven concluded that this creature, with his graceless movement and exposed flesh, would score lower than Steven on the Survivability Scale, a measurement tool he created for the occasion. Steven, without deliberation, scored the match Steven 1, Frog 0, and his mood lifted.

For reasons unclear to Mouse or Frog, Steven shared his assessment.

"I say, my friend, forgive me if I come off as too blunt, but you appear to be easy prey. You have no fangs, your movement is clearly labored and slow, your flesh looks like it could be pierced by even the dullest of teeth, and your appearance is not repulsive, at least in the way necessary to ward off potential predators. Suitors, yes, but predators? No."

Frog smiled the smile you see when one must suffer foolish fools. The smile dropped into a straight line, lips sealed, and an intensity clouded Frog's eyes. His concentration moved inward, and his sagging middle section ballooned, a tightness firming his skin like a large, round drum that would produce the lowest of low tones if struck.

He continued to grow, doubling, tripling, maybe quadrupling his initial contour. His concentration moved outward, and his fierce gaze, leveled directly at the trembling pair, followed them as they sunk into the morass, wishing they could melt into the marshy earth.

Frog's head tilted heavenward, his mouth ripped open, and a scream that could burn the hair off a coyote flew out of it. Unsuspecting birds perched in the branches above were sent scrambling into the air, not knowing what they were fleeing from. He turned towards the pond and exploded, his muscular hind legs fully extending. With a pleasing ker-plunk, he knifed into the water and submerged beneath the mirrored black surface. When Steven and Mouse lifted their heads to see what had happened, taking a deep breath, a rancid smell burned their nostrils.

Deep, loud laughter skimmed off the pond's surface like a slung stone being returned to shore, smacking them in the head, mercifully distracting their sense of smell. They looked towards the laughter and saw Frog's head rising above the water, near the pond's edge.

"Let this be a lesson, bird—learn *before* you speak." A sly grin crept at the corner of Frog's mouth. He was enjoying this moment. "I'd hate for you to see your end because you, how did you put it? Come off as too blunt?"

A low, rumbling chuckle sent rings rippling in the water, emanating from Frog's impressive body. He turned toward the pond's center, and with one powerful stroke of his hind legs, he was halfway there, before his head submerged once again, and he was out of sight.

CHAPTER FIVE

All the Creatures Longed

"HEY, C'MON, LET'S get a move on to the place with falling seeds," urged Mouse, back on task as soon as Frog's head went under, as if the episode didn't happen. He tugged at Steven to get him moving, spinning away from the pond and into a mess of weeds.

Steven followed absently, pondering and hopping despite his own better, hard-earned judgement. He was moved by Frog, a strange, new sensation for him. He had experienced life as a lone traveler on one-way streets. The oncoming headlights required a level of attention he was unaccustomed to.

In Frog, he witnessed mastery like he had back in the Nest, as older birds soared through the air, defying gravity, diving, slicing, banking at incredible angles, and landing abruptly, perfectly. Frog's skills were not a bird's skills, but they were no less beautiful, no less impressive. His talents were adapted to the world he lived in. Steven could sense a peace in his expression of those talents, of being his fullest, best self. His confidence was braided with contentment, making it unbreakable.

(Frog practiced the Four Boxes of Peace. He spent time each day strengthening his values, caring for the health of his responsibilities, growing qualities that improved his well-being, and removing those that impaired it.)

Steven concluded this must be a state for which all the creatures longed. This conclusion did not come easily for Steven, because an audience was not required for Frog's brand of peace to be achieved. He was correct in believing that Frog was Frog, no matter the company. His strengths were his strengths, and his peace was his peace. Developing a strength that wouldn't also bring some level of notoriety seemed like a wasteful pursuit to Steven, but he decided to keep an open mind.

"We're almost there," squeaked Mouse. Steven's stomach had remembered it was starving, and the gurgles became squawks again. Mouse stopped a few feet from the base of a young cedar tree and declared, "This is the spot!"

As if on cue, a seed fell on Steven's head, causing him to wince and shrug his shoulders at the surprise. Luckily for Steven, it was just a tiny millet seed.

"Jackpot!" Mouse blurted, without an ounce of amusement at seeing his friend hit in the head by a seed.

As more seeds began to rain down, Mouse hurriedly set about gathering as much as he could, making a tidy mound of assorted, tantalizing seeds. Steven's interest, despite his now raging hunger, was in discovering the source. Seed collection, and more importantly seed eating, could wait. *Where are these seeds coming from?*

He looked up, and there, hooked on a low branch, was a long, cylindrical bird feeder. It was blue in color, with wire mesh siding and several round openings, each with a short peg protruding from it. On two of these pegs were birds. They were also blue in color, larger than sparrows, and engaged in rapturous conversation while sampling the seeds that filled the feeder to the top. Steven was transfixed.

"My Dear, I do believe this is the finest I have tasted! What a wonderful combination of seasonings! Dare I say ingenious, bold even? The chef is to be commended. They have outdone themselves this time!" Mr. Jay plunged his beak back into the feeder to get more, relishing each mouthful, his energetic movements swinging the feeder, sending more seeds to the floor where Mouse continued to gather with fevered intensity.

Mrs. Jay was measured in her assessment. "I believe that, while quite tasty, something is missing. A glaze, maybe? I don't know, but I'm not convinced this meal deserves the high praise you are bestowing. Good, yes. Great? I believe I've had better."

The gray upon her blue made it appear she wore a sweater.

Steven couldn't stay silent for a second longer.

"Why, hello there!" he bellowed, calling to the pair. "You speak of food in ways I have never heard. Seasoning? Glaze? I am quite taken by the seriousness of your evaluation. Is food something more than mere nourishment?"

The Jays, unaware they were being watched, heard Steven's call, faint from the distance. The seeds cracking in their beaks made it nearly impossible to hear anything. They stopped chomping to take in the creature interrupting their meal.

"Would you like to join us for a nosh?" Mr. Jay asked Steven. Mrs. Jay rolled her eyes, knowing he used words like nosh to show off. Steven couldn't wait to use the word himself, even though he wasn't entirely sure of its meaning.

"I'd love to, but I can't," replied Steven.

"Are you in a rush, young man?" Mr. Jay inquired, feeling curiously spurned by Steven's rejection.

"No, that's not it at all," returned Steven, although he knew Mouse, still collecting seeds and unaware of the conversation taking place, would not welcome a leisurely stay. "I cannot fly," he continued, "so I am unable to join you up there at the feeder."

"Oh no, then you must be injured. My poor, poor dear," said Mrs. Jay reflexively, and the warmth in her tone made Steven think she must be a mother. "Do you need our help to regain your mobility?"

"I appreciate the offer, I do, but I am not injured. I have chosen not to fly. I am a walking sparrow, the first of my kind."

It was as if a silent grenade had exploded, stripping the air of sound waves. Only breathing could be heard in the breather's ears, and those ears were stuffed with cotton. Mr. and Mrs. Jay sat stunned, motionless. The swinging feeder came to a rest. Steven sensed a rush of oncoming traffic was on its way.

"Unless my eyes are failing, you're a sparrow, is that right? So, you *must*," asserted Mr. Jay, "possess the gift of flight!"

The force of Mr. Jay's judgement was fueled by the intense feeling of incredulousness that was boiling within him. His quick assessment was he had never encountered such an absurd statement. Logic followed he had never encountered a more absurd creature.

Since he had retired from teaching, he felt freer to communicate in ways he often wished he could while working but didn't. His tongue had become callous over the school terms from how frequently he had to bite it in the presence of a student, their parents, or an administrator. Mr. Jay, however, had no job he could be fired from. Steven was not his student. His parents were nowhere to be found. He continued.

"Do bees not make their honey? And beavers not their dams? Would you deny us of your pearl were you a deep saltwater clam?"

This is the down-dressing you get when a retired professor is free to speak with impunity. Steven wasn't sure why, but he felt thoroughly naked.

Mr. Jay's roiling energy urged him to continue the rhythmic tongue-lashing, but his mind calmed enough to catch him before he continued. He had said enough. Any more would be wasted, he argued to himself. This foolish creature was unworthy of any further attention.

The silence returned, as Steven had nothing to say. He had stalled on the side of the road. No excuse materialized in his head for him to dress up in fancy clothes and parade about. Instead, he wished there was a rock he could tunnel his way underneath and hide indefinitely. Once there, he would have the freedom to ponder the questions that appeared like bruises on his brain…

What is a beaver?
Or a clam?
And what about these things they make?
These pearls? These dams?

"Come dear, let's depart," said Mrs. Jay to break the spell, "I heard there's a new feeder with seeds that conjure bechamel." (A couple from France had recently moved to a nearby home, and their seed creations had the local bird community buzzing. There was sure to be a long line as they did not take reservations.)

Mrs. Jay had been a doctor before she and Mr. Jay retired and set out on their tour of highly rated bird feeders. Her profession required her to maintain her cool, and it came in handy when her husband got a little hot. In unison, they launched from the feeder, the force of their departure swinging it wildly, seeds spilling out. Mouse bustled excitedly until every seed was accounted for in a pile to be taken to their home.

CHAPTER SIX

The Mind Goes Swimming Deep

"WOW, STEVEN, THIS is quite a score!" exclaimed Mouse, his excitement tempered by his ever-present focus on what to do next. "Let's grab as much as we can and head home. We are going to feast tonight!"

"And for weeks to come," Steven mumbled to himself as he scanned the piles Mouse had made. He set about collecting as many as he could, his wings serving as large surface areas to scoop and hold more than Mouse was capable of in his skinny forelegs.

Mouse, inspired by Steven's carrying capacity, found the largest leaf he could, laid it on the ground, and piled it with seeds. He grabbed the ends, joined them in his forefeet, and hoisted the makeshift carrying sack over his shoulder, losing remarkably few seeds in the process. They began the journey home.

Steven kept the tiniest speck of attention on Mouse, enough to keep on his tail as he led the way. The rest of his attention went inward. He found himself again in that daydreamy walking sleep, where the body moves on instinct while the mind goes swimming deep. He reminded himself that he was alive, a young bird alone in the world—again with the word bending—who could figure out how to survive. He could make it on his own, he believed, and this acknowledgement helped repair his confidence that had taken a beating. But a thought kept nagging, like a shoe with a small stone. The repairs kept being delayed.

Is this all there is? he wondered. *Is this all there will ever be? Find food. Go home. Eat. Sleep. Get up and do it again, and again, and again.* He was confused. It was only his first day away from the Nest, but something in the air signaled it was a true question, an honest one that needed consideration and an answer. Or maybe a submission.

What was it that would signal life was not just idly spent? The answer was not going to come to him anytime soon, and he knew it.

They made it home safely. Steven hadn't noticed anything on the way, his mind detached from their surroundings the whole distance back. Their arrival meant there was work that required his attention. Steven rejoined the here and now.

"We can put our loads down and take in smaller amounts," said Mouse as he dropped his seed-filled leaf. Steven opened his wings and let the seeds fall to the ground, and they took turns taking in as many as their dwelling's narrow, curving entrance would allow. Somewhere in the process Steven was reminded of how hungry he was by his noisy stomach, having not eaten since he had left the Nest. Anything that prompted a thought of the Nest was becoming a mild form of torture.

Once the seeds were in and organized, they enjoyed the meal of a lifetime, one they would remember forever. They were two young creatures in their own home eating meals they gathered and prepared themselves, without the help of any adults. There's no seasoning or glaze that tastes as good as your first hard-earned meal on your own. They both, feeling safe and present, allowed themselves to relish this moment, get drunk on it even. They needed this meal more than for its nourishment of their bodies.

Their bellies grew and grew as if the seeds contained yeast, delicious round loaves of sourdough bread growing inside them. Mouse started a belching contest to relieve the gas buildup, Steven gleefully joining in. The wild giggles that caught hold of them, the kind that are impossible to stop once they get started, meant burps weren't the only noises of gas relief heard by unsuspecting creatures that crept by outside. At times, it sounded like the beginning band of the local high school was warming up, but just the horn section, the pitch and duration of the horn blows dependent upon the body position of the blower, their contortions becoming more elaborate as the evening progressed.

(Mouse found that by sitting on the hard surface of their home's packed earth floor and lifting his right cheek just so, he was able to control his tooting much like a trumpet player. By evening's end, he had become quite masterful at rhythmic, staccato blasts of his "horn." Steven's feathers had a muffling effect, giving his contributions a slurry, downtempo quality, sounding like a trombone being played by someone under the influence of extra-strength nighttime cold medicine.)

If there was ever a chance this meal was not going to be remembered, it got blown out into the freshly fouled night air somewhere in the middle of their improvisatory jazz session.

The following days held to the same pattern—food, home, eat, sleep. On days when their food supply was ample, they never ventured out at all. A restlessness was growing in Steven, a desire to get out and explore for reasons other than to collect the next meal. He kept pushing Mouse to break from the pattern, but he always refused. Steven knew not to push too hard.

While nobody was going to use words like caring or giving to describe Steven Sparrow, his heart was not stone. He was grateful that Mouse had taken him in, and he did understand that his friend may never be free of the Great Attack. Steven never asked twice. He feared, however, that a day would come when he wouldn't even ask once.

CHAPTER SEVEN

A Desire to Partake

ONE DAY AS they headed out to gather seeds—their store was dwindling to less than a week's worth and this concerned Mouse—Steven caught the faintest whiff of a tantalizing new smell. Mouse may have caught it as well, but only Steven responded to it. Not satisfied with a whiff (and who really is?), he overtook Mouse and assumed the lead. Bread had just been baked, and cheese had just been churned. A desire to partake of each in Steven fiercely burned.

As Steven sped up his pursuit through the wispy grass, Mouse nervously in tow, the smell became thicker, pungent and powerful. Steven's desire to eat something other than seeds, to devour the source of these sumptuous smells, became ravenous. If he were a dog, there would have been a sloppy stream of slobber wetting the path and anyone that got close.

They came to a clearing in the grass and the smells reached their peak. So too did the anxiety engulfing Mouse, as he stopped dead in his tracks, his whiskers turning white from the shock. In the near distance could be seen a human home.

"We must go now!" Mouse stammered. He grabbed Steven by the wing and started moving quickly in the opposite direction.

"No way, you maniac!" Steven screamed, jerking his wing from Mouse's grip.

Total darkness engulfed them, as if they had been plunged into a vat of thick, sticky tar. It was a scratchy burlap sack that did it, a sack abruptly, jarringly gathered and swooped upward, swinging to and fro, the jostling inducing not just nausea but a paralyzing panic that spread to them both. There was no purging what seized them.

"I knew this place was bad!" screamed Mouse with a horror that shocked Steven. "But you wouldn't listen and now we'll die! And it's because of you!"

Steven could not believe Mouse would express himself to anyone, let alone Steven, with such fury, such hatred. The rawness of his outburst was hard to witness. It was as if he had been turned inside out, and every drop of pain and fear that lived deep inside of him was now visible in all its grotesque ugliness, dripping like black, molten wax from his exposed skeleton. Steven was being coated in it as they tossed about.

"This is where the cat lives!"

There it was. For a moment, Steven could not breathe. It would be a while before Mouse spoke again.

The swinging and jostling stopped, and the bag they were in plopped onto a hard surface. A new wave of anxiousness washed over them. There was a squeaking noise, hinges thirsting for oil, and then a flash flood of light banished the blackness, and they shrunk in terror. They were blind, and their limbs were pressed firmly against their bodies by thick bands. They were lifted out of the sack and moved through an unfamiliar space, the smells making Steven imagine all of nature had been stuffed into a shoebox. Eventually, they were tossed onto a hard, plastic surface. The rusty hinges squeaked again, and a latch engaged.

Steven's eyes made their adjustments, and he slowly got to his talons. As this new world came into focus, a giant, freckled human face was just a few inches from where he stood. He scrambled backwards, falling and crawling until he could no longer move, hard wires constricting further retreat. He cowered, making himself as small as possible.

"A bird! And a mouse! Just what I needed for my zoo!" squealed a boy with yellow teeth and a messy red hairdo.

CHAPTER EIGHT

A Healthy Silence Filled the Room

THE BOY BOLTED from the room, because as excited as he was at the new additions to his zoo, there was fresh bread and cheese to be had. Nobody in their right mind passes up fresh bread and cheese, no matter how alluring the alternative may be. At least, that was the boy's line of thinking. It had been Steven's too.

The room was a musty, wooden shed, the interior walls unfinished. The exposed studs and tattered tarpaper were interrupted by makeshift shelves holding a forgotten mess of repurposed jars and coffee cans full of nails, screws, and washers, much of it rusted. Steven, righting himself after waves of shocking events, took in the scene. He made sure to avoid setting eyes on Mouse's face as he scanned the room.

There were dirty, oily benches all along the cobwebbed walls, all topped with cages and containers housing creatures small. Across the room were two glass tanks full of murky water, with barely visible silver fish sliding about, bumping up against the glass wall, becoming momentarily visible before disappearing.

An emotion stirred within Steven at the sight of the fish, and for a moment, he felt like he *was* a fish in dark water that had invisible walls he kept bumping into. He couldn't name what he felt, but it hurt to hold it in his mind. He worked to dispel it. Over time, Steven had become skilled at dispelling uncomfortable things that popped up inside of him. Near the fish were several cages, with a ferret, rat, and guinea pig all looking in Steven's direction.

At the far end of the bench his cage was on, there was another glass tank full of water and tiny eyeballs with tiny tails that swam about. Steven would learn these were polliwogs, the baby form of frogs, and his appreciation for the wonderful creature he met near the pond would grow deeper.

Next to that tank was a defeated-looking gray-brown lizard in a glass container all by himself, twigs and rocks haphazardly strewn about the sandy floor to make him feel at home.

The two nearest cages—similar in size and condition to the one he now shared with Mouse—each had a creature attentively observing Steven. In the next cage over was a squirrel. The squirrel was standing at the edge of his cage furthest away from Steven to be near the creature in the next cage over, a rabbit.

The squirrel was orangey brown with a long, bushy tail that wiggled like a rhythmically challenged belly-dancer. His eyes were stuck in a constant state of mild surprise. The rabbit had a sleek, peppered coat, soft almond eyes, and two oversized front teeth long enough to cut their way through three, maybe four carrots at once.

It was clear to Steven that a relationship existed between the two, their proximity and body language communicating they were more than neighbors. They both, in their undeniably adorable furry faces, expressed curiosity and openness. Since

Steven was now looking back at them, they assumed the time was right to welcome the new inhabitants.

"Hello there," beckoned Squirrel.

Rabbit quietly said, "Hi."

"How'd he catch you two?" asked Squirrel. "Was it the smell of baking pie?"

"No," said Steven in response. "I think it was fresh bread and cheese." For a moment they escaped to dreams of sweetly scented breeze.

Mouse was oblivious. In fact, much of the time immediately surrounding their abduction and deposit into the Zoo would be absent from his memory. The tape recorder had been turned off, short-circuited more accurately. He would only ever know of this moment from the accounts of others, if he were to know it at all.

He was huddled in the corner and extremely small looking, smaller than Steven thought possible. His body was convulsing, but at such a high frequency and in waves so small that he appeared still. But Steven could see it. That thing he felt when looking at the fish began producing a ring in his ears. He worked to dispel it again, annoyed the first attempt didn't hold. If he looked at Mouse or thought about him, he heard it.

His only friend in the world lay wrecked on the bare plastic floor of a cage, and it was Steven's doing. Mouse, who had saved Steven's life, was trapped in a state closer to death than life, and it was Steven's fault, and he knew it. The ringing settled into a high-pitched hum.

"What's with your friend?" asked Squirrel.

Steven wanted to explode. *IT'S NONE OF YOUR BUSINESS!* is what he felt like screaming. But he stopped himself. It was an innocent question, not made from judgement or in jest, but everything in Steven's head had him on edge, twitchy and quick triggered. He needed to get out of his head, so Steven turned and looked in his direction, and Squirrel began moving across his cage to be closer to Steven. His tail danced behind him and Steven did his darndest to fight against its entrancing qualities.

"It's not as bad as it appears," Squirrel continued, moving his arms about to concede to the shed's dilapidated appearance. "The food we get is decent, and we get it twice a day without fail. The cages, while not ideal, do provide a sense of safety that none of us ever felt out there. They get cleaned regularly as well, and you won't find that out there."

He was trying to help, and Steven was grateful. He softened to his new neighbor that he just seconds ago felt like tearing into. A quarter smile crept onto Steven's face as he watched Squirrel's tail dance and thought of what to say.

"My friend has history with a cat, and he believes it comes from this place. That cat destroyed everything that was important to him. The scar it left behind is so deep inside," Steven paused, "that I don't think it will ever heal."

Steven knew he was responsible for some of Mouse's scar tissue as well. He kept that to himself.

After Steven was done responding, a healthy silence filled the room. The ringing returned, only now it seemed like Squirrel and Rabbit heard it too. All their eyes settled on Mouse for a time, with only the ringing in their ears to keep them company.

"It's true there is a nasty cat," Rabbit said through gritted teeth, breaking their moment of shared silence. "Nobody in this world, not even my worst enemy, would I wish to cross paths with such an evil creature."

CHAPTER NINE

Into His Stained Brain

SLOWLY AND DELIBERATELY, Rabbit began to detail the story of her encounter with the cat. Steven could tell that it was not a story she wanted to tell. She told it from a sense of duty, for she had been the sole survivor. The recounting of the day's events put Rabbit back in the middle of the terror. Even though much time had passed, the wounds were not healed, and probably never would be.

But as hard as it was to get out, sharing this history dispersed it, diluted it. It was no longer concentrated inside her alone, the others allowing Rabbit to be a little less burdened, a little lighter by accepting a piece of her weight and burying it somewhere far away.

Rabbit was much younger then and the newest member of the Zoo. It had only been a few days since she had been captured while out playing with her older and much faster cousin. There were only a few creatures at the time, and Rabbit was the only one left from that day, making her the longest tenured member of the Zoo.

Cat had gotten into the shed through an open window and began toying with the creatures, hissing and clawing at their cages, enjoying the panic it was causing. Then, one by one, it killed the other creatures, toppling their cages, slashing them with its claws, and seemingly just for the sport of it. Rabbit could swear the first kill, a vole, was unintentional, but it triggered something in Cat that desired more. It didn't eat any that it killed. It didn't drag or carry any of the bodies away. It wasn't run off by the boy, instead choosing to stop when only Rabbit was left alive.

The cat looked about the room, taking in the carnage. It looked at Rabbit with elsewhere eyes and a satisfied grin before sauntering out through the open window that had been closed ever since.

It took Rabbit a long time to get the entire story out, pausing often to catch her breath and calm her nerves. Her voice was never steady. The images she described were like blood-red stains on her brain that would never come clean.

Steven was experiencing déjà vu. As he listened to the horrible events, he couldn't help but think about Mouse and the Great Attack. The details and their impact were so similar that time began to feel like it had chosen to go back.

Could this be how all cats were, killers to their core? Or were these tales of one cat with a twisted taste for gore?

In each tale, one creature was left behind, and their paths had just crossed. The trauma they shared was equally horrific, each losing the only family they had at the time.

Steven was grateful Mouse was in shock, that nothing of this story had made its way into his sizeable ears, into *his* stained brain. Steven felt a responsibility to keep this story from Mouse, to save him from even more pain. He had been a terrible friend to Mouse, hurt him deeply, selfishly, and he needed to start fixing what he had broken. He saw this act as a first step.

Steven was glazed in his pondering, the whining hum in his ears coming and going as thoughts filtered through his head.

Squirrel, partly to move on to lighter fare, partly out of curiosity, inquired of Steven, "Excuse me, but if you don't mind me asking, how did a bird and a mouse become friends? I'm assuming you are, of course, friends, that is, seeing how you were brought in in the same sack and deposited into the same cage. The boy must have been able to capture you in the same swoop."

Steven heard the question but remained in his glaze. The incessant hum was getting to him, and any restraint he started the day with was used up. Unfortunately for Squirrel, Steven decided to release some of the pressure building up.

"As a matter of fact, I do mind you asking. Can't you see this is not the time for such questioning? My friend here is in pain, my *new* friend over there has just shared an obviously traumatic experience—my sincere condolences to you and those you lost, dear Rabbit—and you want to inquire about the origin of a partnership? Have you no decency?"

Steven was not about to share that he found himself in this position because of a choice he made. He was done explaining himself, justifying who he was. Creatures needed to accept him and stop thinking they knew better.

Squirrel, not wanting to seem indecent, offered an apology.

"Apology accepted," said Steven, and that was that.

CHAPTER TEN

A Chance to Lay It Thick

IT WAS CLEAR a break was needed, that space and time needed to be wrapped around everyone like worn, warm blankets that comforted and protected. Squirrel didn't require blanketing, but everyone else did, so a quiet day of reflection was the agenda forced upon him. He didn't mind and was used to it as a woodland creature in a cage by himself.

Mouse remained in shock, catatonic and small in the corner. He was curled up tightly, a light gray ball, his position unchanged for a day and a night. Steven was preparing himself for a hurricane of rage once Mouse came to. In fact, he looked forward to it, needed it. He wanted the wind and rain to blow him across the cage, thrash him about, leave him slumped and broken in the corner. Broken *looking* would be sufficient upon further consideration

"Where are we?" asked the gray ball, waking Steven from his half-sleep.

The room was dark, and the strangeness of waking in a new space for the first time lingered before ecstatic relief washed over Steven, catching him by surprise. Mouse was talking to him!

"It's a zoo," replied Steven, rushed and giddy, getting to his talons and trying to keep his cool. "That strange-looking human, that boy that brought us here, is the keeper. Apparently, his caretaking skills bring about great joy."

Mouse chewed on this last thought, and Steven knew immediately in his flustered attempt to smooth things over he'd gone too far too fast.

"Joy? For whom?" Mouse replied, a question dipped in acid.

Steven remembered the hurricane of rage and thought maybe these were the first winds kicking up. Now that it was approaching, he wasn't so sure he wanted it to make landfall. Maybe he could calm it or redirect it.

"Well, yes, there's that. He, the boy, that is, most likely experiences the greatest pleasure from this little operation here, seeing as he can come and go as he pleases. But I do have it on good authority that, all things considered, we have it pretty good. The food, served twice a day and directly to our dwellings, no foraging required, is of a respectable quality, at times even delicious. These sturdy wires and the greater wooden structure, provide a double layer of protection, which as you can see," Steven paused to sweep his wings around the darkened space, acknowledging the slumber being enjoyed by all the creatures present, "allow for a deep, refreshing sleep that is uncommon in the wild. I've also, in our short time here, come to appreciate that there appears to be a fine community of creatures with very neighborly attitudes and admirable conversation skills."

Mouse began to unfurl and take in the broader scene. All the creatures in their cages slept, the mood was quite serene. The shed's windows, streaked with old water stains and dusted with fine, shifting patterns of dirt, glowed with the first hints of a new day. Through them, and the scattered cracks in the shed's siding, the sun began to stream, moving from a whisper to a scream. The quiet night had ceased, and the stirring of creatures began.

"What about the cat?" asked Mouse.

While Steven was a gifted improvisor, he was grateful to have had time to rehearse for this performance.

"No, it does not live here," he replied without pause and a face so straight you could have plumbed a door frame to it. "According to our new friends," who Steven was grateful were still asleep and out of earshot, "there was one that meandered onto the property once, some time ago. It was a mangy gray-black monster with a severed tail, but it was scared to high heaven with a rifle and hasn't been seen since."

The spirit of a rifle crack went blasting through their minds, for it was the sound that haunted all the hearts of creaturekind.

Steven, not one to pass a chance to lay it thick, was proud of his performance. He knew the addition of the rifle bit, a late revision to the script, would add gravity to the piece. It would connect emotionally with his audience; his story made more believable by its detail. Steven also thought using Rabbit's descriptions of Cat would allow Mouse to believe his demon had been vanquished—if in fact it was the same cat, which he suspected it was from Mouse's reaction to mention of the severed tail—affording him some calm.

Steven knew applause was not the appropriate response, but Mouse's blank stare was deflating. *Oh, well,* Steven thought to himself, *not all great works are appreciated in their time.* He believed, however, that he had done the job he set out to do, which was to move beyond talk of the cat. He gave himself a mental pat on the back.

CHAPTER ELEVEN

Not So Skilled a Drinker

THE SUN'S ARRIVAL meant stretching and yawning were to begin. Furry butts moved towards the ceiling as front legs reached for the farthest wall. Jaw hinges stretched to their widest possible angles. Spines made U's and S's, and a peculiar but oddly pleasant vocal music accompanied the choreography.

Boy bounded into the shed, closed the door behind him, and the freshly warmed-up bodies bounced about their cages. The energy surged to a frenzy. Creatures moved about excitedly in anticipation, sloshing and wiggling and yipping and yapping.

Boy efficiently began distributing food to every creature, bowls and trays filled and swung about, doors and hatches unlatched with one hand, food placed while creatures respectfully backed away, then everything closed and returned and tidied. Mouths gobbled with an intensity that would move the viewer to believe it had been days, weeks even since Boy's last rounds.

It had, in fact, just been hours, but the need to get excited about something is deeply embedded in all creatures' DNA.

Creatures in a zoo just have fewer things to choose from. As a result, feeding time is a popular choice.

"I'll be back later!" Boy shouted as he raced out, securing the door behind him. The creatures didn't register his exit, as passionate gobbling was still in full swing. One by one the bowls and trays were emptied, water slurped, bowels moved, and the drowsiness of full bellies permeated the Zoo.

To Steven and Mouse, it didn't seem like a long enough time to be awake before going back to sleep, but they were learning quickly that the rhythms of life in the Zoo were different from those in the wild. Eating and sleeping were major events in the Zoo, and if you weren't doing one, you were probably doing the other. What else was there? Before long, a symphony of snoring instruments began their mid-morning performance.

Sometime in the afternoon, many of the creatures started stirring, and not long after, Boy came back. His return was met again with excitement, but food was not the reason this time. This was cleaning time, which meant some of the creatures would be moved to temporary quarters while Boy removed the collected filth, replaced the shredded bedding or water, and gave the whole dwelling a good rinse.

While the creatures feigned resistance to the move, to prove to each other they were still wild, it was an act. The true meaning of what it meant to be wild had faded away a long time ago, like a weather-beaten poster that had been hung outdoors and forgotten for seasons, the event it announced now just faint, ghostly splotches on rippled and tattered parchment. Deep down they enjoyed the process because it meant, if just for a moment, they were held.

As most of the creatures were alone in their containers, physical touch was not a regular occurrence. While they never talked about it, they loved the day their home was cleaned, and not for the obvious reason of an emptied commode and fresh sheets. They were moved with care by bare hands. If they were lucky, their back or head received a few strokes along the way. If they did decide to talk about it, they wouldn't know what to say. It wasn't something their stunted language had a capacity to convey.

Steven became impressed with Boy. He believed him to be genuinely in favor of the creatures' welfare, wanting to do his job well for the sake of their well-being. He was careful and diligent, and he never once abused his position of power.

Creatures occasionally behaved in a way Steven saw as ungrateful, considering all they were receiving free of charge, but Boy never made them pay for their transgressions. He would get scratched by flailing nails, pierced by snapping teeth, or soiled with waste, but he never got angry. If anything, he became more caring, more attentive, understanding the offending creature was experiencing a frightful moment and needed some space to let it pass.

It was during the post-cleaning afternoon when Steven got to know his neighbors. After a proper nap and the excitement of cleaning time, the creatures were awake and engaged in social time. Boy usually left during this time, freeing up the creatures to extend their attention elsewhere. Being in cages meant you were limited in who you got to know, and luckily Steven and Mouse's cage was nearest Squirrel's, the most talkative of the bunch. Steven was grateful their cage was not between the polliwogs and Lizard.

Rabbit was just on the other side of Squirrel but close enough to talk to without the need to shout. Lizard was on the other side of Rabbit and would at times join in, but the distance and his glass container made it challenging, Rabbit and Squirrel needing to relay to Steven what Lizard had said like an old-school game of telephone. The ferret, rat, and guinea pig across the shed also seemed to engage in afternoon chats with each other, but they were much too far away for Steven to get to know. They waved at each other if their eyes met, but that was about it.

As the routines of daily life in the Zoo began to fit Steven like the comfiest pajama set you've ever owned, he reflected on his luck in escaping the harsh and deadly wild, albeit unintentionally. He did not know how hard life was until he felt it soft, and easy was a way of life he'd always held aloft.

The comfort and safety he now felt as a pampered member of Boy's Zoo cast a harsh light on life outside of it. Fear of predators and the scarcity of food were only the beginning of the laundry list of hardships experienced by those not lucky enough to be selected for inclusion in an all-expenses-paid, as near to resort-style living experience as any creature was going to get.

But while Steven settled into Zoo-life, thrived even, Mouse struggled. It was clear to Steven that Mouse did not share the high praise he had for Boy or the Zoo. Mouse was no longer catatonic—he did eat modestly, and on occasion he would chime in on the social topic of the day—but Steven knew this was not the Mouse he became friends with. This was not the Mouse that had become his brother, that had saved him, that coursed with an electricity that made it seem he would live forever. The light wasn't out, but it was dim.

He told himself to give it time. Mouse was a simple thinker, and with the complex wines of life, not so skilled a drinker. As far as Steven was concerned, this was the privileged, high society all creatures yearned for, but it required a certain intellect to fully understand and embrace its complexities. Mouse would need to be given time, lots of it, to come fully on board and understand how good he now had it.

Steven was willing to wait. It gave him something to look forward to, which was hard to come by in his new life.

CHAPTER TWELVE

A Symbol of Excellent Living

AFTER SEVERAL MONTHS of life in the Zoo, Steven was thoroughly in tune with the prevailing behaviors and attitudes of his new society. The stretching and yawning, the voracious eating, the indulgent and restorative sleeping, and the time-stretching conversations were actions Steven was becoming exceedingly excellent at.

The fact that these were shared activities with his exclusive new group of friends intensified his enjoyment.

One day during feeding time, Boy placed a shiny metal bucket of feed near Steven and Mouse's cage. It had been some time since Steven had seen a reflection of himself, the last time being when getting a drink in the pond the day before being selected by Boy—he no longer used the word "captured," seeing how his attitude about his situation had evolved—and what he saw then was very different from what he saw now.

At the pond, what he saw was much trimmer, slimmer, and more capable of activity than what peered back at him currently. The image before him resembled an extra-large scoop of Rocky

Road ice cream that had been dropped on the sidewalk and was beginning to melt. A tiny sugar cone beak and a couple chocolate chip eyes completed the picture.

At first glance, he was startled by the change, but as he broke away from the bucket and scanned the room, looking at the physiques of his neighbors, he recognized a kindred dedication to enjoying the Zoo's perks to their fullest. Larger than normal middle sections were the norm, and if one were to be honest, a symbol of excellent living.

Extraordinary contours were only possible if one had access to regular, extra helpings of food coupled with the ability to peacefully lay around for long stretches. This was not possible by his poor brethren in the wild who had to fly far and wide to find food, escape from predators at all hours, and sometimes go days without nourishment or rest. How could they ever retain the calories necessary to grow such an impressive middle? Sadly, they couldn't.

One day Steven was woken from his mid-morning nap earlier than he would have liked by a rhythmic pitter patter and a thumping on the ground. His heavy eyelids were nearly impossible to lift—especially now that they spent more time down than up—but when they did, he witnessed a whirling Mouse in a sea of tranquility. He was running and jumping and pushing and pulling, with an occasional climbing and descending thrown in for good measure. He was non-stop motion in a room where all was still and, beyond Steven, oblivious to Mouse's revolutionary choice to exercise.

Steven halfway believed he was still asleep, a horrible dream ruining a perfectly good nap, his first of the day. Steven had enough when during one of his cartwheels, Mouse unwittingly let loose a stream of sweat that splashed Steven in the face.

"What has gotten into you?" asked Steven with a snap. "Can't you see you woke me from a precious daily nap?"

Mouse paid no mind. Steven had spoken loudly and clearly enough to be heard, but as far as Mouse was concerned, he had spoken nonsense. Pure gibberish. Mouse continued his exercises with a look on his face that was different from those worn by others in the Zoo. Different, even, than any worn previously by Mouse.

Steven studied it, tracking Mouse as he moved about their cage. It had been a while since Steven had seen anyone with that steely look that comprised many emotions in one, desire and focus primary among them. There was a power humming just below Mouse's surface. This wasn't survival, the look familiar in the wild. It wasn't the glazed grin of guiltless pleasure so popular in his new digs either.

He had to go back to his Nest days, when some of the older birds were advancing their flying skills, competing with one another, pushing each other. That may have been when he'd seen it last. *No*, he now remembered, *that wasn't the last time.* Father had it when he told Steven and his siblings it was Flying Day. That's the last time he'd seen it.

CHAPTER THIRTEEN

A Chasm Was Inserted

MOUSE KEPT IT up, the vigorous exercise, the measured eating. Steven could see the improvements happening, not just in the fitness of Mouse's body, but also in his mind. His mood had lifted, and while there was still distance between the two, mainly because Mouse never got fully on board with the luxurious behaviors favored by the Zoo Crew—Steven's name for the clique that included himself, Squirrel, and Rabbit, with Lizard as an associate member—Steven appreciated that Mouse was no longer the sad sack he was when they first arrived.

Mouse had also taken up a modified meditation ritual. He would sit still for long stretches, eyes open, quietly contemplating the entire space of the shed. He would move positions within the cage, sometimes climbing up a side wall to do his practice from a higher vantage point, but always the slow, meditative scanning. His head would move in micro-increments, his eyes intensely focused, as if he were trying to discover something, as if something were hidden somewhere in the shed and it was his goal to find it.

He was quiet during these searches but deeply thoughtful, at least by Mouse's standards as Steven perceived them. Steven, while incredibly intrigued by Mouse's odd behavior, could not imagine anything fantastic was firing in Mouse's brain. Steven didn't waste time wondering what was going on with his friend, his days being as full as they were with eating, napping, and conversing, but it was a curiosity he couldn't let go of. He wanted to inquire, but it didn't feel right, which was an oddity for Steven.

Mouse's exercises continued to become more complex and challenging as his skills and strength improved. He was running faster and jumping higher than Steven thought possible for a mouse, and he now included the entirety of the cage in his routine. He would jump onto a side wall, scurry at different angles to the top, and then hang from the ceiling by his two front feet once he got there, dangling with a grip so strong he had the confidence to dangle on purpose.

The dangling later became pull-ups, many of them, and the climbing back down the way he came became launching dismounts, first from close to the floor heights and eventually from the ceiling. Launching and landing evolved too. Maneuvers in the air like twists and flips were worked on and perfected. Mouse wasn't always successful, as he took a good tumble or two, but it never deterred him. He always got right back at it and worked until he figured it out, and always with that look on his face.

Steven's naps were routinely interrupted. He was tolerant at first but found himself becoming increasingly annoyed at the precious sleep that he was being robbed of. If Steven were being honest, which was rarely a given, it wasn't so much the lost sleep that annoyed him—it was that Mouse's exercise was extending his time awake.

Being awake with nothing to do, while everyone around you was enjoying another glorious trip to Dreamland, was eating away at Steven's quality of life. This is how Steven framed the situation. He briefly recognized that questioning his quality of life as a creature in a zoo was also a possible way to evaluate things, but just like junk mail, he tossed it in the rubbish the minute it arrived. His erosion of life quality was Mouse's doing, and Steven had had enough.

Mouse had just landed an impressive double back flip from the ceiling. Steven hit boiling.

"What exactly are you up to?" Steven shouted, more wildly than he intended. Some creatures stirred and rolled over, but no one woke.

Mouse paused his activity. He never looked down upon Steven. His friend was making choices he would not consider, but that was his right. Mouse owned his life and Steven owned his. Each were using the strengths they had developed to squeeze the best out of each day. Ever since they got to the Zoo, however, their ideas about what made for a Good Life had diverged. That can happen in a relationship when you no longer need to lean on each other.

Mouse figured it was time to update his curious friend on how his definition had evolved. He owed him that respect. On second thought, his definition hadn't evolved at all, only his surroundings had. Steven, he realized, was the one with a fluid definition of *good*. Mouse eventually decided to update Steven of his plans and let him interpret them as he may.

"I am going to escape," said Mouse, a calmness in his voice. "If I'm ever going to live my life, it is the only choice."

There was a truth in Mouse of the likes he'd never seen, and suddenly a chasm was inserted in between.

With a nod, Mouse returned to his exercises. Steven, wanting nothing more than to join everyone else in Dreamland, sat motionless, stunned. Mouse, from the beginning, had been nothing but honest, no falseness in his bones. Steven had dismissed him as simple and easy to read, as easy to be manipulated if that was your thing, as someone who needed to stay in the shallow end of the Pool of Life.

Steven, meanwhile, had always believed himself to be a capable and skilled swimmer no matter what the depth. In fact, the deeper the better. By this analogy, Steven was clearly the winner, something that always mattered to him. Now that he was awake in more ways than one, he was starting to see flaws in his thinking. That hissing noise in his ear was the air beginning to leak out of the flotation devices he hadn't noticed were strapped around his wings.

Steven was a master of the games that creatures play, like knowing the right ear to bend and exactly what to say. These games weren't beholden to the truth. Steven was seeing what happens when you stray too far from it or ignore its existence entirely. Mouse, from the start, clung to the truth like a mountain climber to their rope, and that was why they were responding so differently to life in the Zoo.

Steven was using his skillset to secure a comfortable space within the Zoo, a space where his skills could be utilized to gain him the recognition and privilege he desperately needed. The truth was not something he considered, even for a moment. Mouse rejected the space entirely. It didn't support the truth as he understood it, so it wasn't a place that could support him. He *needed* to escape.

If Steven were being honest, which he was for a change, the scoreboard read Steven 0, Mouse 1.

CHAPTER FOURTEEN

The Ease of Things Made Free

STEVEN'S BRAIN WAS on fire, and he couldn't sleep. He could hear the deep, healthy breathing of Mouse from the other side of their cage, along with all the other wheezes and toots that popped and fizzled throughout the night from various corners of the Zoo.

This wasn't the cause of the fire, nor was it the full moon taking advantage of a cloudless sky, streaming through the high windows, or the buzz of the filters that kept the water creatures' environment from becoming overly murky. No, these things happened every night, and they never kept Steven awake like he was tonight. No, this was Mouse's fault.

I am going to escape. If I'm ever going to live my life, it is the only choice.

This was what started the fire, and Steven repeating it over and over in his head was what was keeping it alive, feeding it the oxygen needed to keep growling and growing, devouring Steven's rationalizations like dry, dead wood. Every reason, every excuse, every straight-up lie reduced to ash as soon as he uttered it.

I am going to escape. If I'm ever going to live my life, it is the only choice. Nothing survived the scorching truth of this simple declaration, and nothing could put it out.

Steven gave up trying to extinguish it. He tried to understand it. If he was capable, accept it. He knew that was a lot to ask of himself in a night, but what choice did he have? He had fallen victim to the ease of things made free, but this too was a lie, for there always was a fee. He was paying that fee now, as he laid there awake, an overweight and lazy walking bird inside a cage, inside a shed.

He had really taken to Zoo life, became good at it. He loved every bit of it, ravenously devouring each portion of his day like it was his favorite donut. But just like a donut, when it was eaten, what next? Another donut, of course, and then another, and another. He was chasing donuts, and it showed in the fullness of his belly and the emptiness of his soul.

If not another donut, then what do I want?

Sometimes, when the truth reveals itself to you, it's all you can do to keep yourself from falling apart. The nature of the falling depends on the nature of the truth and where you stand in relation to it. For Steven, it was a good, deep cry, quiet and alone in the dark. He heaved from the stifled sobbing, and his body sweated like it was working out poison. It was part of the process, the falling, a reset that helped you find your way back.

Steven had never thought beyond the moment, beyond the next transaction, and all he ever wanted in those moments was to end them with him winning, 1-0, according to rules and standards he established and could rewrite as needed. He wasn't tethered to something bigger, something more important than the moment, something more important than himself. He had no rope and was falling.

As the sobbing slowed and as acceptance of the truth began to warm and calm, he thought about his family, the first time in a while since he had done so. He wondered where they were, and he wondered if they were thinking about him. He drudged up memories of their time in the Nest—Father's thrilling flying exhibitions, Mother's caring meals, wrestling with Brother and Sister. He also thought about that last day, when he walked away in a fit of defiant rage while Mother and Father were gone. There weren't many left, but a few more tears soaked the soft, tiny feathers of his face.

He drifted off to Dreamland, and a sensation moved through him, like a rope tightening around his waist, securing him.

CHAPTER FIFTEEN

I Believe Enough's Enough

MOUSE'S EXERCISE HABITS, along with his long stretches of focused mental exertion, translated into the soundest sleep of his life. Night after night, he was falling asleep without worry troubling his mind. His bones and muscles sang with beautiful achiness. He woke each morning with his heart brimming with hope, strange considering where he was waking up, but where he was waking was not as important as where he could potentially be sleeping that night. Each day could be the day, and that's what made each morning so special, so welcome. At the very least, he knew the work he was going to do today would increase the chances that if today wasn't the day, then tomorrow could be.

Today, however, was going to be a very different day indeed. Normally, Mouse was the first to wake in the Zoo, at least among the land creatures. All the other land creatures never seemed to be in much of a hurry to greet the new day, and their stretching and yawning would often drag well beyond necessary to be ready for their first activity of the day, which was eating, followed by a nap. This morning, he was not the first awake. Steven was, and he wasn't just awake, he was exercising.

He was alternating between jumping jacks, laps around the cage, and what appeared to be abdominal crunches. Steven's lack of abdominal strength, however, combined with his rather gelatinous middle, meant little more than his head lifted off the ground. The effort was tremendous despite the minimal movement.

"Good morning, Mouse!" he said, between his deep, exerted huffs. "If you don't mind, I'll join you. I believe enough's enough."

CHAPTER SIXTEEN

The Best of Creaturekind

IN THE WEEKS following Steven's change of heart, when he stopped chasing donuts and joined Mouse on the path to a more self-determined future, they became the kind of brothers one might find, when searching for examples of the best of creaturekind.

They pushed each other to be their best, better than one can push themselves alone. There was healthy competitiveness, for the desire each day was that they both won. They shared a common goal, and the power of working *with* someone to achieve something *together* was strange and awkward for Steven at first. He had worked *alone* and *against*, but not in ways that were obvious to those he found himself pitted against, which was everyone.

He began packing those old attitudes away, tossing them into the windowless attic of his mind along with the scoreboard and locking the door for good. He was moving into a new room, a bright and airy space downstairs with doors that didn't lock, where everyone was welcome, and there was no scoreboard to be found.

As comfortable as Steven became in his new mindset, he still marveled at how he found physical work joyful. He didn't jump out of bed and into action like Mouse did, but the time it took each morning to convince his muscles to get moving became shorter and shorter. Once he started, he always wondered what took him so long, because it felt like guzzling a large glass of hummingbird nectar once he was huffing and puffing. That sugar rush of discipline didn't wear off the whole day. He and Mouse now did everything together with energy he'd never committed to anything.

He was still in the Zoo, but Steven felt a satisfaction that made being awake not just tolerable but fulfilling. Being awake and working with Mouse were now his favorite things in the world, and it was all because he moved rooms in his head.

Pushup after pullup after squat after crunch, with steady progression, the flab melted, and muscle grew in its place. As his strength improved, so did his zeal for obtaining more. He was walking a mile in Mouse's shoes, and he was revising his misguided judgement.

They both knew the goal they set for themselves was a tremendous one, one that required incredible strength, cunning, and luck. They were up upon a bench, inside a cage, inside a shed. The obstacles were many in the path that lay ahead. There was great risk involved if they failed, but once the vision of life beyond the Zoo had materialized in their heads, had become something real like a memory that just hadn't happened yet, there was no risk too great that would make them turn back.

Steven had doubts though. There were brief moments, usually in the short space between laying his head down at night and sleep stealing him into its restorative realm, when Steven questioned whether he was made for this.

Is this my story, or am I just following Mouse off a cliff? That was fear teasing him, playing chicken with his future. A box of donuts would be served up too: a leisurely morning, eating without care, long, luxurious naps, and meandering conversations that went everywhere and nowhere. *What do you say we make that tomorrow's agenda?*

Steven admitted it was a tempting offer, and it would be so easy to do. But he hadn't forgotten how he felt after one of those days and how he felt at the end of a day working with Mouse. *Thanks for the offer, but I'll pass*, he would say, before sleep took hold of him and kept him safe.

Their physical fitness had improved beyond the ability needed to get themselves out of the Zoo, but they still had no idea how they were going to make that happen. No escape route had been discovered, despite all their scanning and scheming. They looked for cracks wide enough they could both fit through and doors or windows that may be ajar or easily opened. Nothing.

In the back of his mind, Steven knew that Boy had taken extra precautions to prevent Cat or any other wild predators from getting into the Zoo ever again, in the process making it impossible for those inside to get out. He kept these thoughts to himself, but he knew they were true. He tried to lock them away in that dark and dirty room with the scoreboard as soon as he could, but somehow, they kept sneaking out.

Despite this nuisance, Steven continued to wholeheartedly move forward with Mouse, the thrill of their pursuit too intoxicating to abandon. He had faith that something would present itself, an opportunity to be seized. They just had to be ready when it did.

CHAPTER SEVENTEEN

The Red Flood

STEVEN'S CHANGE IN routine raised eyebrows (for those that had them). Squirrel and Rabbit, who'd become quite fond of their Zoo Crew membership, were wondering if Steven was exploring a phase, or if this was a new, permanent course of behavior and their afternoon chats were forever down a member.

Squirrel was missing Steven's participation in their group. While Rabbit was his oldest friend, and Lizard was a good chap by anyone's definition, neither were chatty. They weren't mute, but unless one spent many hours in their presence, one could make a mistake that they were.

Steven had brought robust social interaction to Squirrel's life, and he wasn't aware he was desperately needing it until Steven and Mouse's arrival. Steven's ability to fill the air with a steady stream of tales, anecdotes, observations, jokes, and philosophical explorations meant Squirrel did a fair amount of listening, much more than he ever had. Steven did leave space for Squirrel to participate, but there was never any doubt it was Steven's show.

Squirrel didn't mind playing a supporting role. He liked to talk, but it didn't spring from a need to hear his own voice. It was how he connected with other creatures and gathered energy. Steven's absence left him feeling low, and it bothered him.

At first Squirrel thought Steven was joining Mouse in the exercises to reconcile with his housemate. It was clear that some rift had happened between Steven and Mouse prior to their deposit in the Zoo. It was also clear that Boy had no intention of separating them—there were no free cages now, nor a flat surface to put a new one. So, repairing whatever was broken between them was vital if day-to-day life were to be bearable. In Squirrel's estimation the relationship was beyond mended, yet Steven made no attempts to balance time with Mouse and his old buddies in the Zoo Crew.

There were also no attempts to increase the Zoo Crew's membership by bringing Mouse into the fold, an idea Squirrel fancied. Squirrel was exhausted trying to carry the conversations with Rabbit and Lizard. He had run out of things to say. Until now. He nervously mobilized the courage to interrupt his neighbors.

Mouse and Steven were in a planning session, their backs to Squirrel's cage.

"Excuse me! Steven! Mouse!" called Squirrel in their direction.

Steven and Mouse looked at each other before turning to see Squirrel at the wall of his cage near theirs. He was upright, his front feet grabbing the cage as if he needed extra support. Steven and Mouse weren't sure why Squirrel needed to interrupt them, but they had a hunch. They could see that Rabbit had moved to the side of her cage nearest Squirrel's, her attention focused on the conversation about to take place.

"What are you two up to?" Squirrel inquired.

Steven and Mouse turned to each other again and made a few cryptic gestures, but they failed to make a sound to each other or in response to Squirrel's question.

After an awkward pause, Squirrel realized an answer was not coming. He continued. "You have been running and jumping and climbing and scheming, lost in deep thought, or maybe that's just daydreaming?" There was defeat in Squirrel's voice, as if he knew what the answer was, or that it was going to be something he didn't want to hear.

The bit about the daydreaming meant he still had hope that his gut was wrong. He wanted to offer an alternative he was willing to accept without question, although he knew it wasn't true. It's like when a parent asks their teenager to return the car they accidentally borrowed from the driveway.

Steven and Mouse looked at each other again. He had asked it. Their hunch was right. The ensuing conversation between Steven and Mouse was nonverbal—subtle eye shifts, face contortions, arm and leg gestures, and modifications in body orientation. Steven and Mouse had joined forces to execute a covert operation, so they had developed a complex ability to communicate without words being uttered, words that could be intercepted and used against them. It wasn't that they didn't trust the other creatures in the Zoo, it was that their mission was so sacred that there were no risks worth taking.

Mouse, for his part, argued this fact through serious expressions and closed body positions. He believed the mission was a private matter that needed to stay within the dangerously porous walls of their cage. Steven, through more elaborate gestures that had his wings and eyes pointing to various locations about the Zoo, his body communicated he was more open and receptive to the idea that they may need help executing their mission. They still had not crafted a plan that was plausibly executable, and he argued that bringing in fresh perspectives could open possibilities they hadn't considered.

They could trust Squirrel and Rabbit. They could serve as extra eyes and ears, a support team providing intelligence and advice as they made their break for the wild.

After a pause where Mouse went deeply inward before responding, it was agreed to share their mission with Squirrel and Rabbit. They turned to face Squirrel, who was still grasping onto his cage, his shoulders even droopier than before. Steven addressed his beleaguered friend.

"We're preparing to escape; our time here is done. When we've settled on a plan, we're making our run."

Squirrel and Rabbit, now knowing what they had feared, could not keep their faces from contorting into comical cocktails of horror, shock, and disbelief, with a splash of anger mixed in. Squirrel's gyrations signaled a verbal response was bubbling to the surface and would erupt soon. Rabbit looked like an Ice Age creature that had witnessed a horrible scene just before an avalanche froze her over for an eternity.

"Have you gone mad?" Squirrel blurted. His mouth and body continued to convulse to resuscitate an eruption that was not as mighty as he had hoped, but nothing came out. He sunk like a popped beach ball.

While Steven was a changed sparrow, old habits die hard. Or, as is most often the case, not at all. He knew Squirrel was hurt; his words were just words. It was not a statement of fact, it was not a professional diagnosis, and it was not a question that needed to be answered. Mouse communicated a look that said, "Let it go." Unfortunately, Mouse was still in nonverbal mode. He was also behind Steven, out of view.

"I'm glad you asked. If I am to be honest," which Steven was getting much better at, "I believe that we are saner now than ever. The Zoo is simply not the best place for us."

Mouse was relieved when Steven stopped speaking, inhaling deeply after realizing he had been holding his breath. He wished Steven had stuck to the "not the best place for us" part, but he understood what he witnessed was major progress, all things considered. He was proud of his friend for showing restraint.

"What about the cat?" Rabbit had thawed.

Every muscle in Steven became rigid and tense, except for those responsible for moving his beak, the two halves of which began pressing against each other, each trying to snap the other clear off. His brain scrambled to think of something to say to end this conversation, but before he could, Mouse clicked into verbal mode.

"What was that?"

"The cat," replied Rabbit. "What about it? That thing's an evil killer, has a nasty taste for blood. That's why the day I told you 'bout, I call it the Red Flood."

"Told who?" asked Mouse. "I have no memory of you telling us anything."

Steven's beak continued its grinding, and his brain continued its death spiral, failing to pull up the software necessary to end this nightmare.

"I shared it with Steven on that first day. You were still huddled in the corner, in shock. I figured you didn't hear anything, but I just assumed Steven would have shared it with you by now, especially 'cuz you had a similar experience. Any chance to escape, which I feared is what you were up to, is a suicide mission. That cat is outside, I know it. I sense it every day."

It was probably good that Steven was detached from reality now, stuck in his head and only vaguely aware of life beyond his beak and feathers. His internal computer was crashing. A virus he ignored, had forgotten about in the excitement of his system upgrade, had made its way in and was threatening to end everything. His eyes were now completely glazed over, his ears only registering the high-pitched whining of his red-hot brain gears spinning uncontrollably beyond top speed, the smoke they produced seeping out through his ears.

He didn't notice Mouse had come around in front of him, stood there seething into his eyes with a look that blended the deepest hues of hate, anger, and disappointment into a fiery black his beady eyes were perfect for displaying. He didn't notice the fist forming in Mouse's right front foot, nor the coil of his body as every ounce of his formidable strength was transferred to that fist.

Steven's body was stiff as it went to the ground like a felled tree. Whether he was unconscious from the blow to the head, or the computer issues he was experiencing is unimportant. He was out cold.

Mouse found his way to the opposite side of the cage, as far away as possible from everyone, and curled up into a tight, gray ball.

CHAPTER EIGHTEEN

He Finally Knew

STEVEN KNEW HE earned it, but it didn't ease the pain, especially as he saw progress pouring down the drain.

He was conscious now but still sprawled out, prone and lifeless looking. His brain had rebooted after an indeterminate outage, and the Zoo was unnaturally quiet for mid-afternoon conversation time. The details of what had passed were materializing, a horribly realistic fiction he kept trying to convince himself was a delusion, a nightmare in the middle of the day.

When he had the power to move, he rolled over and saw the gray ball of Mouse in the far corner, and it was as if it were day one all over. His one true friend was deeply hurt because of something he had done. *Maybe that's just who I am*, he thought to himself. *Steven the Destroyer.*

A light turned on as he looked at his broken friend. It challenged the thought he had just generated. Steven's instinct was to build a wall of fictional excuses, then hide among the shadows that such a wall induces. He reflexively moved towards the shadows, but the light followed him, banishing the shadows before he could get lost in them. What now?

He felt adrift, snapped away from the solid ground he had discovered and established as home. He focused on himself because that was his habit. He always put himself first, so he thought about what he needed to do to get himself reattached, fixed and back on track. Nothing came. He feared another crash was imminent.

His eyes moved back to Mouse, and the light got brighter, hotter.

He got up and stood there, his eyes not leaving his friend. He stared at Mouse, who lay curled in the corner, and he found his balance again. The puzzle-piece island he stood upon began to drift back to the whole it belonged to. He felt an evaporation happening, as if something inside of him was being turned into gas and encouraged to leave. The puzzle piece snapped into place, and he could move again, and he approached Mouse. He walked until he was near the gray ball.

Helping Mouse was the only thing on his mind.

"Why did you keep it from me?" Mouse questioned with a bite. "You know I have a history! You know that wasn't right!" Mouse's position was unchanged. Steven could not see his mouth from where he was standing, but he heard him clearly.

Mouse moved. He slowly got to standing, rotating until he and Steven were looking at each other, a few paces apart. There was no aggression left in Mouse—he had released all of it into Steven's jaw. He was defeated, and he wore the heavy robe of a boxer that had just learned the fight was rigged and he never had a chance.

Creatures like Mouse, with a religious commitment to the truth, experienced these moments with a funeral-like somberness. To them, something died, and a long period of mourning was in order. He readied himself for an excuse from Steven, for some half-cocked rationalization. Steven settled on what to say.

"I'm sorry," fell out of his beak. "I know that I was wrong." And with humility he finally knew how to be strong. He walked up to his oldest friend, extended out his wings, gave him a hug then added, "For oh so many things."

CHAPTER NINETEEN

Sweet Dreams to All

THAT EVENING AFTER dinner time,
Boy tidied up the shed.
All the creatures got the sleepies,
then headed off to bed.

Boy said, "Sweet dreams to all,"
then turned off the single light.
He exited the shed…

but failed to close the door shut tight.

CHAPTER TWENTY

A Most Foul and Bloody Stench

A THUNDERCLAP ROCKED the creatures of the Zoo from their sleep, the sound of a million hammers coming down on a million light bulbs in the rain, the striking and shattering and splattering of a billion pieces of glass sounding as if it were within the shed.

It was.

They scrambled to their feet, hearts pounding a zillion beats per minute, rushing to the edge of their dwellings to look at the ground where the sound came from.

Broken glass and water covered the cement floor, sprawled among them the contorted bodies of several frogs, some barely moving, while others were completely still, as if they had slept through it all. Thin streams of blood were beginning to streak their way through the water, like rivers within rivers. These had been polliwogs when Steven and Mouse arrived, and Steven had marveled at the transformation they had gone through. He had been too far away to get to know them, but it didn't lessen the knifing pain he felt in watching them die so grotesquely.

Something evil, a specter made of all their greatest fears, hovered in the dark, reaching out with long, bony fingers to nudge the chins of the creatures trying to make sense of what they were seeing, directing their attention to where the frogs' tank had been. There, visible in the moonlight, was Cat, a pleasing grin spread across its face from the attention.

"I'm sorry, did I wake you?" Terror surged throughout the crowd. "I guess I should have known that crashing tanks would be quite loud."

Cat was massive, something closer to what a small lion must look like Steven thought to himself. Dad was a bobcat, knocking up the female farm cat before escaping back into the wild. Mom had abandoned it too, learning quickly that what she had birthed was not something she could train or survive. She had given birth to four kits on that stormy night, but only one came out alive. The possibility of love wasn't even considered as she ran into the teeth of the storm, the thunder and lightning less frightening to her than what she had left on that porch.

Cat was gray with streaks of black and a huge mane of matted hair that shot out in each direction from its round, fat face. It was unkempt and brutish, thick and scarred from a life spent at war, one battle taking half its tail. It was obvious this creature knew only combat, lived for it, was kept alive by it. It had no friends, no keepers, no allies. Everyone and everything were an enemy. The only relationship it tolerated was Boy's family, who put out food for it in exchange for it keeping the rodents away, but there was never any contact, any affection exchanged. It was a contract fulfilled, and that was it.

"What have we here?" Cat purred, scanning the room, flashes of recognition as it passed by Rabbit and Mouse. "I do believe I recognize some old, familiar faces. I really hope your missing friends have found their resting places." The entire room had been dropped in amber, slow becoming slower as it hardened. The final scene preserved for eternity.

All creatures' primary instinct, no matter how improbable the odds, is survival. History informed them that Cat and one more would make it out before the amber solidified and made movement, and life, impossible. Nobody was volunteering to be cast in the scene, to let others go before them, holding the door open out of politeness. This was not a polite moment.

Wild minds began their wild actions, as creatures threw their bodies around their dwellings to break free. The nearer to Cat they were, the graver their situation, the wilder their actions. The fact that Steven and Mouse's cage was at the far end of the bench from where Cat was now, bought them a moment to think before speeding into crazy mode.

"I believe I can undo the latch. I've been watching the boy do it," said Mouse, a steadiness in his voice. He had grabbed Steven by the shoulders and spun him around, looking at him eye to eye. While frantic energy coursed through the room, Mouse was unfazed, and this, in turn, calmed Steven.

This wasn't the plan they had come up with, but this was the plan they were getting. They were physically ready to try, and Mouse was letting Steven know he was mentally ready too. Mouse's forefeet on Steven's shoulders and his eyes in Steven's eyes communicated that he believed Steven was mentally ready too. Mouse was taking the lead, as it should have been.

Mouse scampered into action, running to the door, climbing onto the side, then reaching his forefoot to undo the latch. Steven became the lookout, turning his attention to Cat.

A million more hammers struck a million more light bulbs, this time in a sandstorm. Steven could see Lizard limping off beneath a bench, as the shed became engulfed in a most foul and bloody stench. Steven glanced at Mouse who continued to work furiously on the latch, the rust making it difficult to move, the mechanics of its operation a guessing game to Mouse.

Cat had pushed two glass tanks off the bench by wedging itself between the shed's wall and the tanks, nudging heavily with its shoulder, then when enough space was created, placing its hind legs on the wall and pushing with all the bloodthirsty force it could muster. Up next were three wire cages—Rabbit's, Squirrel's, and then Steven and Mouse's—that would not produce dramatic explosions if pushed off the bench. Steven's mind raced to decipher what would happen next as Cat advanced on Rabbit's cage and Mouse failed to make progress.

Cat sauntered towards Rabbit's cage, and with stunning grace and lightness, it jumped on top, the coated wires of the roof bending under its weight. Cat looked down at Rabbit to convey this time would be different. Rabbit was not intimidated, and instead bared her teeth and let out a growling hiss that made Mouse turn his head for a moment before returning to work on the latch. Cat, caught off guard, regained its swagger before rolling its head back to let out a cackling laugh.

"Well, isn't that cute? Some bravery, from a poor defenseless hare. Don't I deserve a 'thank you' for having chosen you to spare?" Cat lingered, as if a conversation was going to be had, but then continued. "I'm sorry to tell you, that was a one-time deal. I can't have creatures thinking I have favorites. No, that won't do. Today's your day, you little furry marshmallow."

Rabbit coiled and launched, every ounce of strength she had left transferred to her hefty hind legs and jaw. Her mouth opened as she flew upward. A rare look of surprise flashed on Cat's face, but not one of recognition that the bowing of the cage's roof and the width of the wires meant that many of its toes had slid through and dangled above Rabbit, inside the cage.

Rabbit's teeth clamped down on several toes and closed with the force of a mighty guillotine, slicing two clear off. Rabbit fell back to the floor of the cage, tumbling backwards and then rolling over onto her side. She opened her mouth, spit out two of Cat's toes and lay there, victorious and complete.

Cat roared a lion's roar as blood streamed from its foot and into Rabbit's cage. It limped towards the wall, dropped between the wall and the cage, and sent Rabbit's cage soaring through the air. It crashed to the ground amid the broken glass, water, and sand, the door remaining shut, Rabbit's limp body inside. Steven did not believe it was possible that Rabbit could have survived the fall, but an unsteady, bulging movement in her belly meant that at least for the moment, she had.

A third toe had been severed, but it was still attached to Cat's left front paw by a few sinewy strings. Cat stepped on it with its right front paw, and with a mighty pull and an agonizing scream, ripped it off.

Mouse unhooked the latch. "Steven!" he called.

This caught Cat's attention, who was more determined than ever to destroy the lives of every creature in the zoo, except for one. That was Cat's only rule—leave one to tell the tale. The blood streaming from its foot, however, had it rethinking. *Maybe everyone should pay?* The thought dashed as it launched onto Squirrel's cage, sending it toppling backwards onto its side, and then launched again in one fluid motion towards Steven and Mouse's cage.

Mouse had been waiting at the open door for Steven who had just started moving in that direction when Cat's body rammed into their cage and sent it tumbling. Their cage sat on the bench where it met the corner of the shed, and it fumbled like an errant football into one side wall and then the other, before coming to rest with the door swinging open from what was now their ceiling.

Cat pounced up on the ceiling with quickness unexpected from a creature that recently lost three toes, but Cat was a warrior. In battle was where it thrived—a few lost toes and blood were not enough to suspend the pure, raw joy it was having. Cat was thrilled these creatures were putting up a fight. Cat was addicted to rage, and it was as high as it had ever been.

Cat began thrusting its front right leg through the open door, its paw stabbing at Steven and Mouse as they darted about the cage to avoid the sharp nails that would produce life-ending gashes if they made contact. A fierce and manic glaze came over Cat's eyes, its jaws snapping incoherently, saliva oozing into the cage from its mouth, blood dripping from the missing toes.

Steven and Mouse moved with gymnastic precision, climbing the side walls when it worked to their advantage, avoiding the claws and the falling, pooling fluids. They were caught in a battle of attrition that didn't favor them. Cat controlled their only exit, and it knew.

"There's no escape for you two, trapped inside this wire jail. I've decided to spare *no one* in this messy, *lovely* tale." The intensity of Cat's stabbing thrusts picked up, energized by the challenge of the agile creatures it pursued. Steven and Mouse were in excellent condition, but they knew they couldn't keep this up forever.

Then like a bolt of lightning, everything was painted white, and the creatures all took pause in this unfair, one-sided fight.

"NOOOO!" screamed Boy as he charged in, wielding a wooden bat, dressed in boots and pj's. He went straight after the cat.

Stomping over broken glass, Boy swung the bat back in his right hand as he lunged towards the action, and then hurled it forward, level with Cat's position on top of Steven and Mouse's cage. Cat needed to survive. It catapulted towards the floor with an eye towards slinking out of the shed door Boy had left open. Cat figured Boy's wild momentum would carry him into the bench, allowing Cat to easily escape in the opposite direction.

A good warrior knows how to survive to fight another day, and the series of events Cat had mapped out in its head had it doing just that. Cat had launched at an angle to clear the bat and land in a dry patch on the ground, free of the water and sand that covered most of the shed's floor. There was glass scattered everywhere, but that would be easy to avoid after landing. Cat *was* a cat, after all. Boy would crash into the bench. This was not a battle lost, but a battle interrupted. Cat would need to complete it some other day. For now, just survive.

When Cat launched, it was reminded of something that it hadn't factored into its calculations: its missing toes, and the blood the severed stumps were producing. It was too late to change the plan in mid-air.

As Cat landed, its left, front leg, the one with the missing toes and streaming blood, slid out from underneath it, causing Cat to roll onto its left side. Cat's body crashed to the floor, and its shoulder landed next to the metal frame of Lizard's tank. A long, sharp piece of glass was still attached to the metal frame. As Cat's massive head slammed to the ground on the other side of the metal frame from its shoulder, the shard entered Cat's neck and made it all the way through to the other side, the bloody tip obscured by Cat's gnarly mane. Cat's legs made flailing attempts to correct itself, to get upright, but eventually fell lifeless.

After crashing into the bench as Cat predicted he would, Boy steadied himself and turned to assess the chaotic scene. Quickly but carefully, he moved to the floor in the direction of Rabbit's cage, gently opening the door and moving his hand inside.

Steven and Mouse stood there, their breathing deep, replenishing the oxygen they had burned. They were silent as their lungs filled and contracted, and they could feel their energy being restored and their hearts settling. Steven kept his eyes on Boy and Rabbit, while Mouse glanced around the room. Mouse saw that the shed door was open and then tilted his head back to look straight up. The door to their cage was dangling open as well.

A plan materialized in his head, one that required Steven to do something he'd never done before.

CHAPTER TWENTY-ONE

All the Courage They Could Find

THE ODDS, WHILE improved, were still not in their favor. Their cage door was open, but its current position in the center of the roof made getting out of it challenging, for Steven at least. If they were to free themselves of the cage, they were still about four feet from the ground, a ground covered in broken glass, water, and sand, and creatures in various states of death or near death. They had just witnessed how Cat fared when jumping down.

The shed door was open too, but who knew for how long. Boy was in the shed, and while his full attention was on Rabbit's survival, things could change at any moment, and closing the door would happen soon after.

Despite everything, Mouse liked their chances. He turned to Steven to share his plan.

"I need you to fly, Steven. *We* need you to fly."

A look of certain terror seized Steven's face after hearing Mouse's "plan."

Mouse continued.

"I can tell that you're scared, but that's ok," said Mouse to Steven Sparrow, "but you have a gift that we need now. You're a flier in your marrow."

Mouse started explaining what he had in mind, a plan that would require all the courage they could find. While Mouse could climb out of the cage, Steven would need to fly out. It was a short distance, and it would provide a little practice and confidence-building for what would come later. Getting down from the cage to the bench top wouldn't be too difficult, nor would the trek along the bench top to its far end, near the open door.

They would need to do all this as quietly as possible to not alert Boy to their actions. If he did see or hear them, then they were sure closing the shed door would be his first act, foiling their escape. Steven was becoming increasingly doubtful. They hadn't even gotten to the challenging part yet.

Mouse still liked their chances, despite the twitches and tremors being produced on Steven's face.

Mouse then shared the final part of the plan, the part that would free them back into the wild. This is where all their training led them. Mouse gave Steven one last reassuring look, followed by a strong embrace.

Despite everything, Mouse believed in Steven. It was his nature to see the good in others, to look past their unfortunate choices. Mouse could separate the creature from their behavior. He did not see others as good or bad, but merely as creatures that made some good and bad choices, that had developed some good and bad habits. Those things could be corrected. His belief in others, in their potential for greatness, was unwavering.

All that truth and trust seeped in during that hug. The twitches and tremors ceased, and Steven's heart and mind became clear and calm. Mouse let go, stepped back, moving his forefeet to Steven's shoulders, and gave him one last nod.

They were ready. It was now or never. Mouse started climbing towards the ceiling.

CHAPTER TWENTY-TWO

A So Far Flightless Bird

AS MOUSE DEFTLY started climbing towards their cage's opening, a year's worth of thoughts began flooding Steven's mind. Mouse's paw reaching into that pile of leaves and pulling him to safety, not knowing at all who Steven was and what he was getting himself into. Sharing his home. Frog and the Jays. The seed parties and all the juvenile nights spent giggling and burping and farting. Forgiveness after being captured by Boy. Forgiveness after failing to warn about Cat. The training, the encouragement, the trust.

The acceptance.

These thoughts leaked into every crevice, every open space, filling the emptiness with the swirling liquid of his memories. The waters of his past rose and rose, and as the blobbing mass grew, it put pressure on a room that had been sealed shut, and as the pressure increased, the seal broke. The door burst open, the waters rushed in, revealing the scoreboard that Steven had spent so much of his earlier life staring at but had forgotten about. He was surprised to see it still working, the liquid distorting and magnifying its image.

Mouse 923, Steven 0.

Steven closed the door, pushing hard against the syrupy fluid, made thick from the denseness of what it carried. The liquid glubbed out through draining holes in the floor that disappeared as quickly as they had appeared, the rooms of his mind rinsed clean from the washing.

Mouse was nearing the opening.

There was no mystery in Mouse, what you saw is what you got, and Steven knew deep down inside, to him he owed a lot. He also knew that if reversed, Mouse would not think this way. He would simply do the right thing, never thinking who should pay.

Mouse reached the opening, climbed out and onto the roof, and gave Steven a look that asked, *Are you coming?*

Mouse's eyes were plaintive as he waited for a word, from his only ally in this plan, a so far flightless bird. Steven was deeply afraid, his every muscle tense with stress, but with his eyes he told his oldest friend, *The answer's yes!*

CHAPTER TWENTY-THREE

They Shot Out Too Quickly

THE SHIFT IN Mouse's expression, the squinching of his eyes, the lift at each corner of his mouth, filled Steven up. The confidence was building, the doubt receding, and the time to act had come. The strength he felt was a new strength, fuller and more capable than any he'd felt before.

It was *we* strength he was summoning.

He crouched his legs and lifted his wings, exploding from the floor, flapping furiously while watching the ground fall away beneath him. It was a marvelous sensation to be flying, until his head struck the roof, disrupting his movement, sending him crashing back to the floor.

Mouse watched it all intensely, quick glances back and forth between Steven and Boy, who was still focused on the floor with Rabbit. The racket from the other creatures was still booming, the frenzy of the night still alive. The noise made by Steven's crash landing was camouflaged by it, and thankfully did not draw Boy's attention in their direction.

Steven looked at Mouse while he lay on his backside, his first attempt at flight an embarrassing flop.

Mouse motioned that he thought it was an acceptable first attempt, pretty good even. *This time, look up, and you'll get it*, he communicated through a glint in his eyes and a nod of his head.

Never once did Mouse make anyone feel stupid. In fact, the opposite was true. In his company you felt your best. You felt appreciated. Your strengths were front and center, and your flaws were accepted but never pointed out. He was the perfect mate with which to tackle such a test. Steven crouched for another take-off.

He looked up this time, clumsily making his way towards and through the opening in the ceiling. He bumped into a side of the opening, and his landing involved a trip, fall, and tumble. His face was now resting on the wire mesh as his beak pointed through it. His eyes were peering at where he had just been. He was outside of the cage. *I flew!* Mouse scrambled over and helped him to his talons. This was a time for action, Steven reminded himself. Thinking and reflection could come later. If there was a later.

You did it! Mouse believed that even in times of action, quick acknowledgements were well worth any small risks they may incur. The boost in Steven's confidence, which would be desperately needed during this next stretch, was evidence Mouse was right.

They got off the cage and to the bench top, Mouse climbing down the side and Steven using gentle flaps of his wings to jump and land with only a few steps needed to regain balance. No face plant this time. *Progress!* They made their way to the wall, hoping it would obscure their movement from Boy's view. He was still focused on Rabbit.

They started moving towards the far end of the bench, staying as low as possible. Up ahead was Squirrel's toppled cage, the solid floor of which had become the side wall facing Mouse and Steven's cage. They hadn't seen Squirrel since Cat launched from his cage to pounce on theirs.

As they got closer to Squirrel's cage and could see around the solid wall, they saw him standing there, his forefeet grabbing the wires, his face pressed against them to see Steven and Mouse as they moved. They paused, the wire wall between them. Mouse noticed his cage door had remained closed in the tumble.

They all stood there in silence, and an unspoken truth passed between them. There wasn't time to free Squirrel from his cage, and even if there was, the final part of their escape was impossible with three creatures. Squirrel wanted them to know that was ok. He wanted to stay.

He wanted to be here for Rabbit when she came around, and he'd been away from the wild too long to miss it. He probably wouldn't do very good out there anyway. Unlike Steven and Mouse, he was in Zoo shape. He would be a liability. He put his forefeet on his belly and summoned a weak smile.

As quietly as he could, Squirrel whispered, "It was great to know you both, now go!" He fought back tears until they had moved on and their backs were to him. Only then did he let them run, hope and pride surging in their waves.

With no more structures to hide behind as they moved along the bench, remaining low and as near the shed wall as possible, they crept at a more cautious speed. The heightened energy in the shed was subsiding. Creatures were beginning to calm down and make less noise. It wasn't yet still and quiet, but Steven and Mouse's movements were becoming more pronounced. Boy's focus was still elsewhere, but they knew their time to escape was running out.

They reached the edge of the bench, the open shed door just beyond them. In the center of the shed was Boy, his knees on the ground as he held Rabbit cradled in his left arm, his right hand stroking her back from head to hind. They could not discern Rabbit's condition, and they knew they couldn't spend time doing so.

There was shattered glass, water, and sand everywhere, along with the lifeless bodies of several frogs. Cat's body was impaled on the glass shard, blood oozing from the rupture. Lizard was nowhere they could see. They hoped he was alive and hiding underneath one of the benches. Maybe he had escaped out the open door.

When Boy had swung the shed door open, the sweep had cleared away the debris that had been there. They looked at each other and agreed that that was the ideal landing space. Going straight down, which is what Steven had imagined they would be doing when he first signed on to this scheme, was just too dangerous. Too many sharp, perilous glass pieces, combined with a bird that hadn't yet mastered flying or landing, created too great a risk. They needed to shoot for that clear space, which would place them at the open door's threshold. From there it was just a dead sprint to freedom.

The vertical distance to the ground was about four feet, and the horizontal distance to their target looked to be double, maybe triple that. Some momentum would be needed to get there. Steven took ten paces back in the direction from where they had just come, away from the door. Mouse knew exactly what he was doing, turning to face him, his back to the door and the bench's edge. By turning this direction, he was able to keep tabs on Boy.

When Steven got the distance he thought he needed, he turned to see Mouse facing him, crouched and in a ready position, forefeet open at shoulder height. It was now or never, and Mouse believed the moment warranted clicking out of silent mode. He looked at Steven and shouted, "It's time for you to save us friend…I believe so much in you!" And with those words of confidence, Steven knew just what to do.

He started running in Mouse's direction while flapping his wings, and as he did so, Mouse squeezed into a tighter crouch. Mouse's scream of encouragement and Steven's running and flapping had caught Boy's attention, and he raised his head to see what was happening. With his eyes now up, after registering who had caught his attention, Boy's focus shifted to the open door. A panic took hold of him as he realized what was happening, and he began the process of getting upright.

Rabbit was cradled in his left arm, and he wasn't about to jeopardize her safety by setting her down, so he covered her up with his right hand as he wriggled to get his feet underneath him. Once on his feet, his boots would protect him as he ran to close the door, but getting to his feet without the use of his hands, not to mention on slippery, sandy ground, was a challenging task. He wasn't moving as quickly as he wanted to.

Meanwhile, Steven's feet had just barely left the surface of the bench, but he had already chewed up more than half the distance he had between Mouse and where he had started running. Steven wished he had counted off twenty paces, but it was too late now.

Mouse couldn't back up because he was at the bench's edge. This was their one shot—adjustments were necessary. Steven's flapping doubled in speed, and he lifted, but now he was too high, higher than Mouse would be standing with outstretched forelegs, but it was too late to make an adjustment down. Mouse was centimeters away, and it looked like their one shot would be missed, or that Steven was going to shoot out of the shed alone, leaving Mouse standing at the edge of the bench watching as the door closed.

Steven stopped flapping and started gliding, and his trajectory dropped a fraction, just enough to allow Mouse—who had realized he needed to time the jump of his life just right to catch his flight out—to launch and grab onto his ankles. He grabbed on for dear life and was swept away backwards.

The momentum carried them beyond the bench's edge, but the added weight and Steven's paused flapping caused them to plummet quickly. They were heading for a crash landing in a sea of broken glass. Steven resumed his flapping at the greatest speed he could marshal, which stabilized their fall, but because Mouse had had to jump and grab, his body was swinging uncontrollably, which made it hard for Steven to fly straight.

While crashing onto glass was no longer a threat, crashing into a wall or the door now was. Steven tried to maintain his flapping speed while adjusting the angles of his wings, eventually stabilizing their flight path. They were headed for the opening.

Boy had gotten to his feet, and Mouse could see the determination he had to beat them to the door. Keeping Rabbit secure with both hands, he started charging, glass popping under his boots as he sprinted. Mouse didn't think they were going to make it. His mental calculations had Boy reaching out and closing the door before they got there, and their inability to slow their progress in time would have them crashing into it.

The thought tracked through his mind to yank on Steven's leg to change their course, to dive to their left and swoop back into the shed. They would avert crashing into a closed door, a likely fatal crash. They would be trapped back in the Zoo, but they would be alive.

Mouse didn't yank, and they continued their path to the opening. Boy was gaining, and only Mouse was aware how close he was. Steven's eyes were locked on their destination. Just when Mouse believed Boy should begin extending his right arm to reach the door to shove it closed, and as Mouse began to assume the universal crash posture of eyes closed and shoulders hunched, something different happened.

Boy kept his right hand secured on top of Rabbit, choosing not to extend it towards the door. Instead, he turned his right shoulder towards the door, and he slowed his pace.

This altered Mouse's calculations. "Go! Go! Go!" he shouted to Steven. Their flight path was stabilized. Steven's flapping picked up. Their trajectory was still downward, but the increased pace had them landing five or six feet outside the door. Both parties arrived at the door almost simultaneously, but *almost* was all Steven and Mouse needed.

Boy lunged to shoulder shut the door, to keep them locked in tight, but they shot out too quickly, fleeing back into the night.

CHAPTER TWENTY-FOUR

Joy Abundant in His Heart

THEY RAN AND ran, then ran some more until they finally dropped, neither of them sure that their emotions could be topped. They did it! They were free! They were completely spent by the time they found a discarded cinder block half buried in the ground to crawl into. The half that was underground was accessed by a short tunnel that some creature at some time had dug out, but the space was abandoned.

It was a large space, and it was kept warm and comfortable by the heat transferred from the half that stuck out of the ground and absorbed the sun all day. Mouse didn't like that the entrance was free of deterrent twists and turns, but it would do for a night, especially considering that Cat was dead.

While their bodies could barely move, their mouths couldn't stop. Their minds were racing, recounting every second of their incredible escape. They needed to verbalize it all, call it back up and verify it for the record. Nothing of this night could be lost, ever. The story needed to be emblazoned into each of their brains, detail by detail, so it could be told, passed on, never lost to history. Never, ever lost to them.

Steven did more listening than he had ever done, and Mouse more talking, but neither noticed nor cared. They were high on their achievement, explosions of remembrance leading to intense rounds of excitement and banter as they hammered out the truth of what happened. They each had sections where only they could share, especially the flight portion as each had been focused in different directions.

Mouse was able to share details on Boy's actions, how close he came, how much care he showed Rabbit while trying to keep them from escaping. Steven shared details on the flight, how he learned to manipulate his wings just in time to stabilize their path and not crash into a wall. Their cheek muscles began to ache from all the smiling and laughing. Their buzz was slowly wearing off, the exhilaration fading.

The pain that had been masked by their adrenaline was beginning to remind them of the physical toll their adventure had taken. It was time to sleep, to repair their bodies for tomorrow's journey to find a new home and start their post-Zoo life. They needed to stop talking and let their brains organize all the details they had just gathered. Mouse had one more thing he needed to share.

"You did it friend. You flew, and because of it, I'm free. I'm forever grateful, Steven. You're a hero, can't you see?" Then Mouse drifted off to sleep with joy abundant in his heart, thankful for his friend, and for a chance at a new start.

Despite the physical pain that was becoming more pronounced, Steven knew he had never felt so good in his life. He knew why, too. His heart had never been this full, and it scared him a little. It scared him a lot, if he were being honest, and he was.

Steven was a thinker, someone that spent his life in the world of ideas and words, and not of emotions. He had become a master of thoughts, could control them, contort them, craft them out of thin air. He felt in control when thoughts and ideas and words were the oxygen being breathed.

This though, what was happening in his heart, he felt less comfortable with, almost dizzy, like the feeling of being at high altitude. He couldn't wipe the smile off his face or keep his whole body from tingling with a joy that felt like he may explode at any moment, tiny pieces of him plastered to every surface of the cinder block. He couldn't control it.

What scared him most was that it could go away, be lost and never found again. He didn't feel that way with thoughts, ideas, and words. The well was endless where they came from. What was happening in his heart was not like that. Maybe what made it so scary is also what made it so great—there wasn't an endless well. Or at least there wasn't one you could access alone.

Steven stared at Mouse, now deeply asleep. He knew that tiny gray ball curled up just a few inches away was why he was feeling the way he did. They had visited the well together. They had put their lives on the line for each other. They had regained their freedom as one.

His eyes began their descent, and every muscle felt like it was dissolving into liquid. This was the greatest day of his life, and he fought to keep it from ending, but it was useless. *Days must end*, he thought to himself, *and that's what makes them special.*

CHAPTER TWENTY-FIVE

In Such a Peaceful State

STEVEN WOKE UP to a loud and unfamiliar snoring, a deep and rumbled pitch that brought to mind a rocket soaring. He opened up his eyes to see a long and sleeping snake that looked like it had swallowed an entire birthday cake.

The acute fear that seized his muscles woke the head-to-toe pain that hadn't fully left his body despite the catatonic sleep he'd just risen from. He didn't move, but he knew that once he did, it would hurt. Being eaten by a snake would hurt too, he reasoned, so suffering a little muscle discomfort would be worth it.

Without moving his head, he moved his eyeballs to the edges of their lines of sight, scanning to find Mouse. No luck. Snake's snoring was so loud that he couldn't decipher whether or not he heard Mouse's deep, prolonged sleep breaths. He knew them well, and he diverted all his brainpower to his hearing to search for it. No luck. All he could hear was Snake. *Maybe Mouse is outside?*

Snake's snoring gave Steven the impression his unwanted roommate was somewhere in the deeper regions of Dreamland.

This was a sliver of good news in a day that had begun with a thunderstorm of bad. As Steven got his bearings, he realized Snake was sleeping in between him and the exit tunnel, prompting another thunderclap to crack in his head. As gently as possible, he stood up.

Going as slow as possible meant more strain on his muscles, all of which reminded him through angry shouts of what he put them through yesterday. He apologized, but let them know this was kind of important, so please shut up. They agreed to table the discussion until later, but they were not happy. Steven thanked them and got to his talons.

There was just enough space between Snake's resting head and the side wall of the cinder block to fit Steven without having to contact either. It would require extremely controlled shuffling, a body squeezed as tightly as possible, and as little breathing as was necessary. Maybe none if he could afford it.

His muscles shouted their disapproval. He shushed them and readied for his escape, the second in two days. Zoo life wasn't looking too bad now.

He started moving towards the space he would need to squeeze through, and because he was so focused on where he was going and not where he was, he failed to see the portion of dried leaf that lay on the ground right in front of him.

To Steven, the sound it made was exploding dynamite. He wished it was. He wanted nothing more than for chunks of cinder block and earth to come crashing down on his head.

"Why are you not up in a tree?"

Snake was awake.

Steven froze and assessed his options. Snake blocked the exit, so his only chance to get out was to fight his way out. He didn't care for this option and rightly believed Snake was more skilled in this arena. As his software moved towards a crash, Snake sensed Steven's fear and prepared to speak again. Snake was used to creatures getting tongue-tied in its presence, so it was well practiced in the art of calming the afraid.

"Please, have no fear, dear bird. I don't intend to eat you. As you can see, I ate last night, and it'll take some days to move through."

Snake had alternating bands of dark and light scales, and its bulging middle made it look like a sumo wrestler persuaded to referee a high school football game. Its eyes were drowsy, and it spoke with a calm sleepiness that could almost be described as genteel were the words not being spoken by a deadly snake. Steven, however, did believe what Snake was telling him. Like Mouse, he sensed an honesty that put him at ease.

This was turning into a very peculiar start to the day. When he had gone to sleep, he had imagined that he and Mouse were going to begin their search for the perfect place to start their post-Zoo life. Instead, he was preparing to converse with a snake. He had no idea where Mouse was.

"It's a long story as to how I ended up here. Maybe some other time." While Steven did not feel he was under immediate threat from Snake, he also had no intention of becoming chummy. He had a day he wanted to get back on track, one that required finding his friend.

He needed to use his tools of rhetoric to get him out of this trap. This realization gave him a little shot of confidence, and his posture improved. He looked directly at Snake and put a gentle, comfortable look on his face, with interested eyes and a half smile.

"I understand your reticence to engage in conversation, I really do," said Snake. "I get it all the time, especially with the smallest creatures. But I can assure you that I mean no harm."

Steven felt sorry for him. Snake seemed lonely, and while Steven was still focused on getting out of there and finding Mouse, he figured a little conversation wouldn't hurt. He didn't want to talk about the escape from the Zoo, however, so he changed subjects.

Steven, feeling safer, asked, "What was it that you ate?"

Snake replied, "A sleeping mouse, in such a peaceful state."

CHAPTER TWENTY-SIX

On Sadness He Got Drunk

STEVEN LAUNCHED LIKE a rocket, half running, half flying, his body parallel to the ground, his talon claws churning and scraping, his wings wildly flapping, all frenetic propulsion with the sole aim of getting outside. It happened too fast for Snake to do other than close his eyes and wait for it to be over. Steven skimmed over Snake's mid-section and shot into the exit tunnel, his chest slamming against the dirt as the tunnel slanted upward towards the light of the sun. His face hit the ground soon after, and his rear end flew up and hit the narrow tunnel's ceiling.

He picked up the flapping and churning again, shooting out of the tunnel and hopping, hopping, hopping as fast as he could, as far away from there as he could get. Flying would get him farther faster, but he wasn't going to fly. He couldn't think of flying. If he did, he felt sick, the kind of sick that made you want to open your mouth as far as you could and not close it again until everything inside of you was out. *Everything*, heart included.

He wanted to move in reverse. He wanted to hop and flap backwards, to slow the Earth from spinning forwards and get it going in the other direction, turning back time. Not far, not even twenty-four hours, just to the middle of last night when Mouse asked him to fly.

NO! he would scream this time at the top of his lungs, enough to get Boy's attention, to alert him to the open door. Mouse would be upset and angry, but he would be alive. *HE WOULD BE ALIVE!*

They would get past it. Boy would restore the Zoo, and Cat was dead. Sure, it would just be more of the same, more donuts, but anything, *anything* was better than this. Whatever it would take to bring back the most important creature in his life, he was willing to do it.

He knew it was futile. There wasn't anything he could do. Mouse was gone, and he was alone and lost. All he could do was hop, and hop, and hop. And sob, and sob, and sob.

He came upon an overgrown thicket of bushes, the ground covered in dead, rotting leaves. The air was musty and damp, with an undulating ribbon of acidic decay. The web of branches and leaves did not allow sunlight to pass through. The place felt like he felt, so he decided to stop hopping.

He looked into the tangled web and knew he could disappear into it, work his way into its center, and never encounter another soul. This is what he deserved, the sacrifice he needed to make so that nobody else got hurt by his actions. He reached and grabbed the lowest branch and pulled himself up, wedging between rubbery shoots, pushing through clumps of leaves, climbing branches like a ladder. He kept going until he believed he had found dead center, a thick, impenetrable wall of limbs and leaves between himself and the rest of the world. A self-imposed solitary confinement for crimes against creaturekind that were unforgiveable.

There was only one crime and one creature that mattered, but for Steven, everything was on trial, and "guilty" was the only verdict considered. He settled on a branch, and leaning back against a trunk, wallowed in the darkness, and on sadness he got drunk. Steven the Destroyer was sentenced to life.

He made a vow to never leave until his time was done. He would stay there in the thicket and avoid the light of sun. He'd live on ants that climbed the trunk, water dripping from the leaves, become the Hermit of the Bush, his only goal to sleep and grieve.

CHAPTER TWENTY-SEVEN

In This Universe They Were Alone

THERE WAS NO mark of time in the bush, so whether Steven had been there a week, or a year, was unknown and of no consequence. As deep as Steven was, no light made its way in. It was always night, which suited what he was becoming. Days were for hoping and wishing, for new beginnings and moving forward. Steven just wanted to sleep.

He was done hoping and wishing. He had tried those things, been duped by their promises, gotten high on their temporary hits of bliss. It was all just a sugar-coated lie, sweet on the outside and painfully bitter on the inside, the bitterness so sticky it pulled your teeth out as you chewed. He knew he could chew for a lifetime and never be finished. He didn't want to finish. Just chew, chew, chew.

Not many creatures called this area home, but the few that did avoided this bush. Even those that passed through on a seasonal basis knew to stay away. The place had changed since Steven decided to crawl up inside and stay there. A transformation was happening.

Without a soul to talk to, without the light to grow, Steven paled until there was no Steven left to know. Mossy twigs and leaves fell into his thick coat of disheveled feathers and planted themselves. His silhouette became spiky and horned.

The stench of stillness grew pungent and tacky, his odor shockingly foul. The other creatures, even those with less than keen smelling, knew in the middle of that bush was something as close to death as a living thing could be.

The legend of the Hermit of the Bush became a thing, about the mean old creature and the bush he ruled as King. It was said that if you ventured in, sadness gripped your soul, that love would leave your body, and your heart would turn to coal.

As night came to those outside the bush, the most daring creatures would gather in nearby bushes, just beyond the stench. These plucky creatures were usually the younger ones, just naive enough to seek a thrill by tempting the most extreme emotions to have their way with them, foolishly believing they could find their way back at will. Sometimes they were there on a dare, sometimes to prove they weren't afraid of anything, and sometimes just to be reassured somebody was worse off than they were.

It didn't happen every night, but when it did, those in attendance would experience something nobody ever came back for a second helping of. It would come wafting out of the bush, wrapped in a fog of pain so damp and so thick that once it wrapped itself around you, seeped into your fur or feathers, you couldn't move until the sun came up and burned it off.

Those that heard it, and had the strength to talk about it afterwards, agreed it was the saddest sound a creature would ever hear. Its icy song left a chill in some creatures' bones that led to weeks, sometimes months of shaking before they could work it out.

Some believed the only thing that could make such a sound was not close to death but indeed dead. It was impossible to fathom a living creature could make such a sound and have a beating heart, let alone a soul.

Most creatures had heard the cry of one of their own pierced by a bullet or arrow, or in the closed jaws of a predator or trap, and none believed those screams to be worse than what came from the Hermit's Bush. Those poor souls were clinging to life as it poured out of them and pooled on the ground. What came from the bush had no reverence for life; it disdained it.

The sound they heard on certain nights, a haunting, howling moan, left them feeling in this universe they were alone.

PART THREE

The Great Tree

CHAPTER TWENTY-EIGHT

Fear Descended Like an Avalanche

SIX YOUNG SPARROWS decided to play dangerously near the Hermit's Bush, primarily because their parents told them not to. They were brothers and sisters and cousins, three of each, and as brothers and sisters and cousins are apt to do, much teasing and daring was taking place.

"You're afraid!"

"No, you are!"

This was the gist of their conversation, exchanged in all its tempos and volumes. When they had run out of variations, they moved onto the next topic.

"You're a big fat poopyhead!"

"No, you are!"

Their parents, the ones that had warned them against venturing near the Hermit's Bush—it was now officially referred to as such—were nearby collecting food. Or maybe they were napping. As parents of young sparrows, they found themselves in a constant state of exhaustion.

They, the two sets of parents that were each responsible for three of the young ones currently engaged in another caper they were warned against, had been caught in an endless loop of "eat this," "stop that," and "play with your cousins while I take a quick nap." Since they often forgot which command they last uttered, they had started acting as if all three had been. Rounds of seed collecting were therefore infused with bouts of napping, which were then interrupted with bolt awakenings and shouts of "Stop that!" upon hearing one of the many distress signals that parents' ears become finely tuned to and capable of hearing regardless of their current state of consciousness or the noise level of the environment.

As capers are prone to, something small and harmless morphs into something large and harmful on the wings of a single, impulsive, and birdbrained dare.

"Are we sparrows, or are we chickens?"

In every group, there is *that* one. The one that fires the first shot or crosses the red line, and in doing so, commits the *entire* group to the consequence of their decision. This group was full of *those ones*, and this phrase was a favorite trigger they all pulled with a giddy, joyful, yet wreckful sense of abandon. It's unimportant to single out which of the spirited hooligans pulled the trigger this time, for it could have been any of them. Truth be told, they may have all shouted it in unison once an impasse had been reached in the Afraid-Poopyhead Debate.

It was agreed that none of them were chickens, so with the intoxicating sense of foreboding they had become quite addicted to, they entered the Hermit's Bush. After pushing their way through the dense skirt of twigs and leaves that extended to the ground, they entered a nearly pitch-black world, the stitchwork matrix of branches above them only faintly backlit from the sun above, the overgrowth of leaves allowing a dim glow to filter through, like a weak flashlight pushing through a dark, thick blanket.

The smell that engulfed them as they made their way in brought a wave of nausea that toppled them to their knees, some authentically, and the others in solidarity. Thankfully they hadn't eaten yet, so nobody expelled anything.

The better sense in them after being brought to their knees by merely the stench of the place, was to exit immediately. They, however, were all caught in a perpetual race to be the cause of their group entering into a caper. *None* wanted to be branded as the one that ended one prematurely. They got back to their talons and pushed forward.

They knew the glory was not in merely entering the Hermit's Bush, but in seeing the Hermit in the flesh. To glimpse the legendary Hermit and live to tell the tale would be to reach a certain immortality, at least in the reasoning of a tween sparrow. Their parents' need for naps was understandable when one accepted this truth.

As they pushed upward through the leaves, grabbing onto branches, talons digging into soft wood, their heads tucked into their bodies to reduce the infiltration of the smell, the difficulty of their mission became a distraction, so much so that they forgot to be afraid. They became so focused on their next step, and on covering their nostrils, that the Hermit had left their minds.

The Hermit, however, had become quite attuned to the approaching sparrows. Beyond the witless insects, no creature had ever entered the Bush. The Hermit was prepared to make sure no one ever did again.

"WHO DARES TO ENTER MY DOMAIN!" The Hermit's voice boomed, ricocheting off leaves and shattering into a thousand screams, pelting the cousins from every angle as if there were an Army of Hermits. They froze in their ascent, all clinging to a branch, and then a wave of fear descended like an avalanche.

"Herrrrrmiiiiit!"

"Helllllp!"

"Ahhhhhhh!"

"Daaaaaad!"

"Mooooom!"

"Flyyyyyy!"

Their cries for help pierced the air, and while it would never be spoken about, many leaves and branches below them received a splattering of their fear. They began a furious descent, not caring what they may be stepping in or who produced it.

Their parents, who were used to cries for help, had never heard anything this desperate or violent. They had also never heard cries from *all* of them. This was different from one of them getting tricked into eating worm castings under the lie that it was a delicacy, the lot of them stifling sheepish giggles while the sucker puked their guts out. This sounded serious and real. Their children were in danger.

Nothing focuses and energizes a parent like having their child scream with authentic terror, let alone their entire brood. All four parents darted towards the Hermit's Bush with ferocious abandon, barreling into the bush, breaking limbs, ripping leaves, and bouncing off branches too thick to be broken by their size and speed. They felt no pain and wouldn't until their children were safe.

The mothers began collecting the children, one by one finding them and shuttling them to the ground and out of the Hermit's Bush. The fathers went on the hunt. Saving their children was not enough for them, as what they heard spill out of their kids had triggered a foolish need for retribution.

All sense had been pushed aside, and they climbed and pushed towards the center, towards the stench, towards the Hermit. They knew they were getting close as their eyes began to water. Then they saw it, the monster that had terrorized its last creature. Their energy was untamed, bold and reckless and capable of taking down an elephant.

The Hermit sat there and waited for his attackers to come. This would be a fitting end, he thought to himself, as time was not working fast enough. He could see that two were coming, fast and hard and angry. He schlumped down on his branch, even more than he normally did. He closed his eyes and hoped that the two killers would be quick, two crushing blows to snap his brittle bones like feeble sticks.

The attackers arrived at his branch, stopping on either side of him. He could feel their angry huffing. He tensed in anticipation, but nothing happened.

He waited. Nothing happened.

Was I hallucinating?

He slowly opened his eyes. He wasn't hallucinating. Two adult male sparrows stood there. One was paralyzed in a state of awe, beak slightly open and eyes wide. The other looked confused, head darting back and forth between the Hermit and his frozen friend. The frozen one shook his head, opened and closed his eyes a few times, wiped them with his wings, and then began to speak.

"Steven…is that you?"

CHAPTER TWENTY-NINE

Like When Your Heart So Freely Sings

"SISTER! SISTER! COME! Come quick!" Brother yelled at the top of his lungs. He remained still as could be except for his beak, his eyes wide and locked on the Hermit. The other male sparrow, his brother-in-law, remained in a heightened state of alert, the adrenaline of their intended attack still coursing through him, causing him to be jumpy and confused with how to diffuse it. He wasn't sure if he should or not.

Sister, huddled with the children and her sister-in-law just outside the Hermit's Bush, heard her brother's call and was shocked by his request. Then panic overtook her as she feared the worst, hearing her brother's voice but not her husband's. Her husband and brother had gotten into minor scraps before, letting their emotions and egos get the better of them. She always worried when the two of them flipped their Big Dummy Switch on at the same time and feared one of these times, the dust up wouldn't be so minor. She left the children with her sister-in-law and shot back into the Hermit's Bush.

As she pushed and clawed her way upward, letting the stench be her guide, her husband's adrenaline settled enough for him to realize what may be going through his wife's head.

"Honey! I'm fine," he called in her direction, his tone apologetic. "We're both okay. But come, come to the center. You'll want to see this."

Hearing his voice settled her and made her realize she was more wound up than she knew. She had been wildly climbing, scraping herself on broken twigs, plowing through leaves. She slowed, became more careful in her movements, but no less urgent. *What could possibly be so important that I need to see it?* she thought to herself as she trudged upward. Her mind drew a blank.

The smell was becoming unbearable as she climbed, nausea simmering, threatening to bubble over the sides of her slowly boiling pot.

"Right here, Honey," her husband called as she neared. "Just a few more inches straight ahead."

She pushed through the last clump of leaves between her and where her husband, brother, and the Hermit stood. It was so dark she could barely make out anyone's features, but she knew her husband and brother well enough to tell which was which. The third figure looked deformed, bird-like, but also otherworldly. Feathers poked out this way and that, many of which needed to be plucked and discarded. Twigs and leaves protruded at odd angles. She had a strong desire to start cleaning him up.

But there was also something very familiar, and it drew her closer and closer until her face was within an inch of his, and she peered into the Hermit's eyes. After a moment of locked eyes, Steven closed his, as embarrassment and shame overcame him. The realization of what Sister was looking at, *who* she was looking at, struck her like lightning, the surging energy causing every feather to feel like it was standing on end.

"Steven, is that really you?" She lunged and wrapped him in her wings. There's nothing in this world like when your heart so freely sings. Steven opened swollen eyes, wider than in years, to see the ones he'd thought he'd lost, and to make room for the tears.

Steven's heart and mind were racing, blood shooting through veins that were near collapse from lack of use. He hadn't moved much or cared for himself at all since he climbed into the Bush, since he had locked away everything that had made him Steven. Since he had become the Hermit. But now the door had been kicked open, light was pouring in, and everything he had tried to forget or bury was waking up. He had grown used to a constant chill, every part of him slightly numb, but the surging blood brought warmth and tingles.

He was too inside of himself to hear exactly what was being said by the three visitors, but the tone was loving, positive, exciting. The tears flowed, clearing all the dirt, debris, and filth that had caked there, matted into the feathers around his face. His vision improved, and he looked in their direction, the disbelief so deep that he was still having a hard time believing he was here, in this moment.

He felt disconnected and elsewhere, tethered to the Hermit and the Bush by a thin string, his body rising away, the other three reeling him in. He wasn't sure which he wanted to be successful. He could see clearly now that all six of their eyes were upon him, broad smiles and wild talking passing between them. Their focus on him meant that they didn't see the fourth sparrow coming up behind them.

"So, Mom, is this Uncle Steven, the famous walking bird? The one that Grandpa talked about that had a gift with words?" A niece with big round eyes hopped on their branch to be nearby. "I thought I'd never meet you and thought for sure that you would die."

"Stevie!" blurted out her mom, then shot her quite a look, as something inside Steven came alive and slightly shook.

Stevie got embarrassed from the scolding and moved quickly to another branch, but she never took her eyes off Steven. Stevie was different from her cousins and siblings, prioritizing knowledge over thrills and giggles. She was acutely curious, often wearing out her parents and aunt and uncle with her incessant questioning. If she was awake, she was learning, which meant her observation goggles were always on.

While the other five were back with her aunt pushing and shoving and teasing each other about who screamed first, she had picked up on the weird vibe the adults were putting off. She had seen her mom leave in a cloud of worry like never before, and had been listening to the faint, muffled outlines of what was being shouted between them in the bush. When her aunt was focused on separating a brother and a cousin, she slipped away to chase after what was going on.

She moved just far enough away to not get any more of her mom's ire, but still close enough to hear everything.

After giving her daughter the stay-there-don't-move-we'll-address-this-later look, Sister turned back to Steven.

"Forgive your niece, Steven. That's Stevie, my daughter, *our* daughter," she corrected herself, pointing towards her husband. "We named her after you."

CHAPTER THIRTY

The Tales That Father Told

SISTER SENT HER husband and Stevie to join the rest of their clan and tell them what was going on. They should also locate a place to bed down for the night, which they believed was coming soon. The current events and the Hermit's Bush had distorted their sense of time. They wanted to help get Steven out of there, but they knew it was going to take a while.

It was obvious he had been there a long time and hadn't moved beyond shuffling on the thick branch he was perched on. Despite the imposing bulk of his silhouette, made intimidating by the matted feathers and once-green matter that had accumulated, Brother and Sister could tell a small sparrow was buried underneath. Small and weak. Steven, their brother, was buried under a pile of filth, and they needed to dig him out.

"I can't believe it Steven. I never thought I'd get the chance—" Brother stopped himself abruptly, averting his glance. He was susceptible to rogue waves of emotion, but his reaction was well rehearsed—look away, find a private area, furiously fight back the tears, casually run a wing past his nose to dab the dribbling snot, and then mention the dust particles in his eyes.

Brother was uncomfortable with the vulnerable emotions, and nobody, no adults at least, bought his routine, but they let him think they did. His many strengths had served them all well. Suffering his stunted attempts to stifle his emotions was something they were happy to do because they were a family. It was beginning to dawn on Sister and Brother that their family had grown, that ten was now eleven. There was so much to get to, so much to do.

"Where are Mother, and Father?" Steven asked in a cracked voice. His look was unnerving, but his voice more so to Sister and Brother. Their Steven, the Steven of their memory, would talk non-stop, and the strong quality of his voice was representative of someone that exercised it robustly. This voice, the one that inquired about their parents, was unpracticed, weedy and frail.

Their response was not immediate. The pause was the answer. Sister broke the silence.

"They lived a good long life, and their grandkids brought them joy, and they talked about you often, their bright, courageous boy."

Steven did not possess Brother's emotion squashing skills. He was swept up in the tsunami, a thrashing wall of emotion tossing him around, every memory of his parents a boulder or uprooted tree caught in the power of the wave, everything crashing turbulently into each other. He didn't fight it. He gave in and let it take him away, torrents of tears cascading down his face, violent sobs rolling through his body, his legs giving out.

The salty water pouring out of him was roiling with pain and guilt and regret.

Sister and Brother went to him immediately, cradled him, and joined him. This tsunami had been building, the earthquake cracking the sea floor when Steven walked away from their Nest. All this time, it had been traveling, subterranean, unnoticed but building in power, under all their feet. Hearing that his parents continued to talk about him, and in positive ways, was what brought it above ground and set it free.

For a while they crouched there, the three of them huddled and sobbing, being cleansed of the caked-on dirt they had all been ignoring, just in different ways and for different reasons. Slowly, the tsunami lost energy and washed back out to sea. They regained their footing. Destruction was everywhere. They needed to find a new place to call home. Without speaking, they started climbing out of the Hermit's Bush.

When they made it to the ground, Sister's husband was there waiting. They had found a safe place to camp nearby and had gathered some food as well. He would take them there.

"I hope you don't mind company—we're really quite a crowd," said Sister with a smile so wide, "and I hope you don't mind loud."

Steven mustered a half smile. Nervousness at meeting his nieces and nephews bubbled in his stomach. Sister put a reassuring wing around her brother, and together they turned and started following her husband back to the camp.

They had traveled just a few paces when Steven stopped, causing the others to trip over themselves. They looked at Steven as he seemed to be lost in thought, and they feared he was having doubts, that this was too much. That he was going to let them know he was going to climb back up into his dark and filthy perch, alone.

Instead, he lifted his head, looked at his sister and brother, and asked, "What do the children really know of me?"

There was a childlike sheepishness in his voice, his eyes worried and nervous. Brother turned to him, reassuringly placing his wings on Steven's shoulders, and looked him square in the face. With the calm and love that Sister had seen him communicate so many times to his children, he spoke to his brother.

"They know the tales that Father told, about his walking son who made a choice to do something that hadn't yet been done."

Steven couldn't move. His eyes became cloudy and distant.

Brother removed his wings from Steven's shoulders and took a step backwards. He turned and continued in the direction they had been going, his sister and brother-in-law following his lead, as if their movement was enough to get Steven in motion. They took a few cautious steps before stopping, anxiousness mounting as they turned to see Steven paralyzed, his hard shell vacant, no signs of life they could perceive.

Steven was trapped in the darkness of his mind, again. The shadows were fighting to retain control, to snuff out the light, to pull Steven backwards, to get him alone. *The bush is where you belong,* they whispered, *it's where you deserve to be.*

Sister returned to his side and put her wing around him. She did not pull him, but just stood there, with him.

"When you are ready Steven, we can go." She knew she needed to say more. "If you'd like to go back to the bush, we can help. It's up to you."

The shadows were quieted as a faint flicker sparked in Steven's eyes.

Sister's resolve held her husband and brother in check, the instinct to grab and yank Steven twisting inside them. They waited in silence.

The flame grew in Steven's eyes, and he glanced at Sister.

He took a step forward.

CHAPTER THIRTY-ONE

A Soul in Need of Deep Repair

AN IMPROMPTU PARTY was happening all around Steven. The children were running about, unsettled and vibrantly alive, the energy surging through them sparked by the joy pouring out of their parents and the realization that the Hermit was their uncle. The parents were all smiles and laughs, and "yes" was their answer to everything. Nobody was getting in trouble tonight. Tonight was a miracle, and nothing was going to spoil it.

Steven took it all in, engaging occasionally with a smile, a head nod, or a quick snort of a chuckle. He was mostly quiet, reflective, in that space just below the surface where the outside world could be seen, but nothing was in focus. The gauzy curtains were drawn for privacy, the ones that still let the light through. The blackout curtains had been ripped from the rod and tossed into the corner.

The light had a cleansing effect, killing the mold and bacteria that had spread all over the walls of his mind. A new growth was happening, something planted in love and hope and nourished by the light. He couldn't help but be a little scared by what he was feeling. The last time he had felt anything near what was happening inside of him now was the last night he had seen Mouse, the night of their escape. The night before Snake.

He wasn't sure why, but the fear he felt was fleeting, whisper-thin and smoky, temporary. It wafted out just as it had wafted in, and he believed his environment was the reason. He couldn't imagine all that he had buried himself under in the Hermit's Bush, all the self-hatred, had a chance to survive in a setting like this, where so many fail-safes were in place to prevent it from happening.

The fail-safes were the family members, all of them dedicated to everyone else. Steven had had one friend, one fail-safe, and he was eaten in his sleep, which allowed Steven to spiral into despair, lose himself in pain until he no longer existed. Until he was nothing but mold, ugly and grotesque.

But that was hard to do when love and laughter filled the air and found their way into a soul in need of deep repair. His gratitude at being found, at being set free from an enslavement of his own doing, warmed his bones that had turned black from frost. The warmth put him in a pondering mood, an old, favorite jacket he hadn't worn in too long.

He glanced at Sister and Brother, both now settled in tight with their spouses, smiling and talking, the ease and joy of their communication informing Steven there was nothing new in what he was witnessing. The children bouncing about, engaging with brother, sister, cousin, mother, father, uncle, aunt. Each interaction was indecipherable from the next, the relationships tight and warm and accepting from so much time together, so many common experiences.

Would I have a family too, and children of my own? The pondering moved quickly into the land of what if, an alternate universe overlapping with his. (A memory sparked two to three times. Blinks of eyes. A young sparrow dusting herself off, the taste of dirt in the back of his throat, eyes peering in and out of grass. It vanished before it could take hold.)

What are the places that together we'd have flown? He couldn't quite wrap his head around where this family of fliers may have been. There was undoubtedly a worldliness about them.

Why did I walk away? He hadn't pondered this question since soon after he'd left the Nest. He'd never settled on an answer then, and one wasn't coming to mind now. He could ponder for the rest of his life and never figure it out. Anything he settled on would be fiction.

Why didn't anyone stop me? This question was unfair, and he knew the second it materialized. Sister and Brother were children, and Mother and Father were nowhere to be found when he'd left. If anything, he had come to know in the hardest ways possible that his life was his doing. He could also admit to himself that if someone had tried, he wouldn't have listened. He knew who he was back then, and he knew that things had a one hundred and twelve percent chance of being carried out once he had set them in motion.

Reflection led to Mouse, and how any change to his past would erase not only his memory of him but everything Steven had learned and become because of his greatest friend. As dark and painful as much of his life had been, the thought of never knowing Mouse hurt more. It wasn't a possibility he could bring himself to ponder.

Whatever good there was in Steven, he believed Mouse was responsible. He saved Steven, taught him, loved him, insisted on the best from him, and never gave up on him. Mouse was honest and sincere. Mouse wasn't just devoted to the truth; he was the truth. Mouse had become, and would always be, Steven's North Star.

As Steven pondered, letting the what-ifs get the better of him, getting swept away in the nostalgia of his time with Mouse, he could hear a familiar voice, squeaky and to the point, begin to speak up.

The past is all and done. Get out of your head and join your family. The present and your future are waiting. You can do it…I believe in you.

Mouse was right, and Steven drew back the gauzy curtains and joined the party. In that moment he knew what to do, how to move forward.

CHAPTER THIRTY-TWO

The Chirps of Early Morning

IT HAD BEEN a while since Steven heard the chirps of early morning or seen the sun reflected in the dew leaves were adorning, but he woke into a technicolor world with open eyes, flushed of all their filth from some deep and cleansing cries.

So too had his head been cleared, locks had been undone, the kind of locks that make one think for options there are none. But now there was dimension, there was depth to all he saw, and he marveled at the hand of the divine, what it could draw.

The children were awake now, and active as kids are, they instantly began to play and tease and dance and spar. The morning peace was lost, and in its place the noise of day, the only day there ever was, until it went away.

He saw Stevie in the distance with her siblings and cousins, a pea just outside the pod. She was a willing participant in their games, but something distinguished her from the rest. She occupied that liminal space between young and old, drawn to the actions of the young because she was young, but participating with the detached perspective of someone much older, someone that wouldn't normally partake in something juvenile.

The others, her siblings and cousins, thrived in their youthful revelry, growing tired and distracted when tasked with more mature demands. Stevie was the opposite, jumping at any opportunity to stretch herself intellectually beyond a snappy comeback to being called some form of excrement.

Steven watched them all play for some time before calling over to her. "Stevie!" he beckoned, her head turning immediately in his direction. "Could I borrow you for a moment?"

The distance between them was short and hoppable, but Stevie chose to fly it, darting through the air in several powerful thrusts of her wings, and then throwing out her talons beneath her, adjusting her wings to counter the thrust, bringing her to an immediate and expertly executed landing, no extra hops required to steady her balance. Her eyes were large and craving as she stood at attention.

"What do you need, Uncle Steven?" she asked.

Now that she was here, now that he had set in motion an idea, the doubt of that idea began to grow like mold on the walls of his mind, walls that had just been scrubbed clean. It was just a black spot on a white surface, wanting to be ignored, wanting the lights to be turned off so that it could grow and cover all the white until none could be seen. Mold was mold, just like scorpions were scorpions, and its drive was its drive. You knew what you were getting when you allowed it in or took it for a ride.

Steven wasn't about to ignore it this time. He knew he would never be free of the mold's attempts to dirty the walls, to turn the clean and pure into something toxic. It would always be there, in the air and below the surface, waiting for its opportunity, but he would be ready and vigilant.

He casually turned up the light and burned it away, watching the smoke of its memory sneak out the window and disappear.

"Can you help me fly?" he asked her.

CHAPTER THIRTY-THREE

He Absorbed the Great Design

THE REST OF the family pretended to pay no notice, to keep their focus on the ground. They pretended to play and collect food and tidy up as if those were the only things that had their attention. The truth is that they didn't need to pretend or keep their distance from each other or do anything other than what they wanted to do, which was to gather into a tight cluster and stare into the sky.

They could have done exactly that because who they would have been watching would never have noticed. Steven and Stevie were entirely focused on the task at hand, and there was no way an enraptured audience, all of them intensely focused on their every move, would catch their attention or distract them.

The lesson stretched on for several hours, Steven tumbling this way and that through the air as Stevie patiently provided guidance and feedback. She was an excellent tutor, skilled at making the complex understandable, assessing flaws and prescribing fixes, and for keeping an even, positive attitude despite the obvious frustrations that come with helping someone that was behind to catch up. Stevie was also very good at building skills, homing in on foundational skills that boost the abilities and confidence necessary for the more complex maneuvers to come.

By the end of the lesson, after becoming adept at take-offs and landings from the ground, take-offs and landings from a branch, turns, climbs, and dives, Steven was becoming comfortable entering bushes and trees at great speed and quickly locating a secluded branch to land on, an advanced evasive technique.

As a final test, Steven shot off for the sun, the highest branch on the Great Tree his destination. His body ached from all the work, but it was a wonderfully welcome pain. After so many dark days (months? years?) of inactivity, his body and his mind were alive again, and his heart rejoiced. He was sure the bass drum thunder of it beating could be heard for miles.

As he climbed and climbed, picking up speed as he went, not wanting to leave any fuel in the tank, the cool wind slicked back the feathers on his face and squinted his eyes, moisture streaking away from their corners. As he neared his destination, he threw forward his talons and stuck the landing. He was higher than he had ever been.

No more than a second later, Stevie was beside him. She was as fresh as when the day started. Steven needed time to recover.

"There's nothing quite like flying through the sky and all that blue," said Stevie as she looked out and enjoyed the stunning view. Steven knew where she had picked up that poetic phrase and smiled as he took in the view that went for days and days.

Until this point, he had lived his life upon the ground, where all you saw was flat, in a world that is quite round. The horizon, from this vantage point, was a gentle, curving line, and he was overwhelmed with awe as he absorbed the great design.

Now that he had adjusted to the height, comfortable in his talons' grip, he turned his focus to the silhouette of the Great Tree printed on the ground beneath them. He knew the area well, had spent his entire life there, and understood the sun's patterns, how and when it arced through the sky, and when those patterns shifted. He recognized now how the Great Tree's shade moved about, how at different times of the day or year it laid down in different sections.

As he traced the shade's movements in his head, seeing all that it touched and would touch again, he realized his entire history lay within its influence. Every action he'd ever taken, decision he'd ever made, and word he'd ever uttered, happened down there. In an instant, his entire life was reduced to a speck of sand. He had never known it to be anything else, but now that he was seeing the beach for the first time, it took his breath away and made him dizzy.

He moved his left wing to a nearby branch to steady himself, and Stevie, sensing what was happening, shuffled to him and put her wing around him. He took a few deep breaths, cleared his head, and regained his balance.

"Stevie, tell me this," he had a notion to explore, "have you in your travels been exposed to so much more?"

"More of what?" she asked, seeking out some clarity.

"Well, more than can be found," he said, "beneath this awesome tree."

She took some time to answer, for she was a thoughtful bird, which often meant her cousins teased her, calling her a nerd. But she didn't mind the teasing, saw it as a badge of pride. She had a knack for thinking deep and saw no need to hide.

"Yes and no," she finally answered, aware her answer needed an explanation she was happy to lay out. "There is a world beneath this tree, containing everything the larger world contains. There is life, and there is death. There is joy, and there is pain. There are friends and enemies, work and play. There are complex communities. Everything, right beneath us."

She paused to lift her head, to look beyond the Great Tree's reach before continuing. "These things are out there too, in different shapes and sizes, but at their core, they are the same. Just as there are patterns in how the shade moves about throughout the day, throughout the year, so too do all creatures belong to patterns. They are recognizable when you observe from a distance, and when you are patient."

She hesitated for a moment before turning her attention to Steven. "You changed your pattern today. Mostly creatures stay in the pattern they left the Nest with. Maybe I'll meet others like you as I get older, but maybe I won't. I have a feeling it won't be many if I do. It feels rare. Not impossible, but very hard, and very hard usually means it is rare."

Birds possess the ability to shift perspective, to see a thing up close, and then to fly far above it to understand its place in the greater whole, to understand its environment. They can see influence and shifting dynamics. They can see the parts of the whole that are growing and those that are decaying. The wisdom their gift affords them is one of the greatest in the Kingdom of Creatures.

Steven was beginning to understand this as he sat with his niece and listened to her. He wondered if the nagging in his brain had been this, an innate tug to shift perspective, to use his gift.

Steven had only looked at things closely, had lacked perspective of anything greater than himself. He was always at the center of everything he looked at, everything he considered and acted upon. He grew up quickly in that moment of discovery. His new pattern was discarding old bits of himself that fell outside of its improved trajectory.

Stevie's response was rattling in his head. He understood some of what she had said, as if she had spoken it in a language different from his, but one built from the same root language. The words were similar but different enough to not allow for full, deep comprehension.

He knew the only way to fully grasp her message was to travel to where the language was spoken, to immerse himself, from dawn to dusk, to listening and speaking it. Excitement surged in him as the world expanded before his eyes.

The eagerness was making him jumpy. He turned to Stevie to settle himself. "I'd like to see more of the world," he said to her, "now that I can fly."

"You always could," she blurted in response, as if it was a topic she couldn't wait to discuss. She looked at him like a scientist observing her subject, full of curiosity and wonder. "You chose not to. Why?"

The question should have stung, but it didn't, because she had asked it without judgement. Or maybe because the part of him that would have felt the sting had been discarded. There was a bit of Mouse in his niece, Steven noted to himself, a devotion to truth. It was comforting.

The lack of sting didn't make it easy to answer. It was *the* question, the one he had asked himself many times and failed to answer. Others had asked and been rebuffed. He began to formulate a response, a reflexive impulse buried deep in a forgotten closet of his mind. He could hear it in the back of his head, the justification, the truth-bending, the aggressiveness. A musty smell settled in his nostrils as he contemplated the response formulating in his head. The answer stood there, dressed in a cheap suit like an ambulance-chasing-lawyer ready to dazzle and confuse.

As Steven stared at it in his mind's eye, the suit fell limp, as if the wearer had vanished into thin air. He shone the light on the empty suit and watched it turn to a pile of ash, a gust lifting and dispersing its fine particles.

"I'm not sure to tell the truth, and it doesn't matter now. I know that I'm ready to fly, grateful you showed me how."

Mouse was smiling.

Stevie accepted it with a nod and then pointed to the ground where their family was, huddled together, all eyes on the Great Tree.

"Shall we join them?" she asked her uncle.

They shared a laugh after Steven turned to see what she was pointing at. With the flair of Olympic high divers, they executed a synchronized swan dive in their family's direction.

After reuniting on the ground, Sister gave him a warm embrace, whereupon the cousins mocked their affection with dramatic hugs with each other, adding loud fake smooches and deep ballroom dips for their adoring audience.

Brother, his size often the only recognizable trait of his adult status, engaged in mock gut punching of Steven once the love fest died down. This inspired a Broadway-worthy street fight to break out among the cousins, a Sharks versus Jets battle to the hysterical, giggly death.

Epilogue

Felt the Warming Sun Instead

That night they made a plan
to leave the Hermit's Bush behind
and travel to the sweetest water
one could ever find.
Brother heard about a lake
a full day's flight away.
They would leave their camp at dawn,
and for a couple days, they'd stay.

Steven found it hard
to fall asleep as it got dark.
The plan was in his head;
he was excited to embark.
But the flying did catch up with him,
and he went out like a light,
enjoying a heavy, restful sleep
all through the starry night.

The next day when the sun came up,
they were in the air.
As far as moments go,
Steven had nothing to compare.
He took a second to look down
at where his life had been,
and began to wriggle from its grasp,
the shedding of a skin.

He saw the hole of Mouse's house,
the bog beside the pond,
the feeder in the cedar tree,
and the shed they did abscond.
The cinder block where he met Snake
and lost his one true friend,
and the dark bush he believed
would be his home until the end.

And just like that, his past was passed.
He was flying somewhere new!
Because he found it's not too late
for some choices to undo.
No longer would the Great Tree
cast a shadow on his head,
as he flew beyond its branches,
felt the warming sun instead.

From the Author

I first wrote Steven's story as an epic poem in metered rhyme. This version is a very faithful, almost verse by verse interpretation of that original tale. In fact, I kept many lines intact. Did you catch them?

I chose to self-publish because I'm impatient. Steven needed to be set free and not sent to languish in inboxes. I would rather you came upon this book during a trip to an independent, brick-and-mortar bookstore. That day *will* come. For now, I hope your online shopping experience was satisfactory.

Social media is not *my* bag, and I avoid most of the activities that would likely increase sales of my work. I love to write, but not to engage in the hustle of selling. (Unless it involves live interactions. Reach out if you'd like me to talk with your group. I've been a middle and high school teacher for over twenty years—engaging with groups is one of my happy places.)

I do, however, hope that many more find their way to Steven Sparrow. I believe his story is important. If you found value in it, could you share that with a friend? Could you post something on *your* social media?

At the very least, could you write a review?

Please let me know what you think about *Steven Sparrow and the Shade of a Great Tree*. There is more Steven Sparrow to come. His journey, like all of ours, has surprising twists in store.

Matthew Dale Jones
March 2025

For Pondering

1. Why do you think Steven chose to walk? Was it ultimately the best decision? What decisions in your past do you still think about?
2. Steven has a talent for choosing words (determined vs. stubborn, selected vs. captured) and justifying his actions. Is this an admirable talent? Make sure to *justify* your answer.
3. Does Steven grow from his encounters with Frog and Mr. & Mrs. Jay? If so, what does he learn?
4. Why is Steven not satisfied with a life on Mouse's terms? What is he afraid of at the end of Chapter Six?
5. Is a Good Life possible within the Zoo? Can you think of any real world "zoos"? Do you have any in your life?
6. Was Steven justified in keeping the Red Flood from Mouse?
7. Is Mouse as "simple" as Steven makes him out to be? Why does Steven characterize him this way?
8. Is anything truly free? Or does everything come with a cost?
9. Steven struggles with doubt. What strategies does he use to overcome it? Are they effective? How do you deal with doubt?
10. Why doesn't Mouse yank on Steven's leg when he believes they will crash and potentially die during their escape?

11. What if Steven and Mouse never encounter Snake—will their friendship last? Will Steven continue flying? Will their pre-Zoo tensions return?

12. Steven likes labels for himself (Walking Bird, Destroyer). What label would you give him at the end of the story? What label(s) would you give yourself?

13. Characters are referred to as having default settings, compulsions, and habits. What are some of yours, both positive and less than positive? Can they be changed?

14. It takes Steven a long time to "undo" his decision to be a walking sparrow. Why doesn't he change his mind sooner? What causes us to become entrenched in our decisions and prone to justification?

15. Multiple characters are living with past traumas. Does it need to be brought "above ground" and dealt with? Or is keeping it buried a healthy option? Can trauma produce strength? Or does it always weaken?

16. When Steven and Stevie are in the Great Tree, the powerful influence of environment (everything surrounding an individual) is discussed. Are we powerless against our environment? What factors in your environment have the greatest impact on you?

17. Mouse modeled acceptance for Steven. Did Steven learn how to apply it to his own life?

18. It's mentioned that a line drawn between Flying Day and any other day in a sparrow's life will make sense. Later, Stevie mentions that what Steven did was rare, that she's never seen anyone change their "pattern." Do you agree that people don't change much?

19. Why is the Epilogue a poem?

20. What is *your* definition of a Good Life? What is it that will signal life is not just idly spent?

Acknowledgements

I will never be able to thank Laurie enough in my lifetime for all her support, gracious enduring of my ramblings, and attentive response to every "I have an idea" that dribbles out of me. Thank you, thank you, thank you. I love you.

I'd also like to thank Stefan (@pwaperpro on fiverr.com) for the super cool cover.

Matthew Dale Jones is a public high school teacher. He was the two-time MVP of his high school volleyball team and is on a mission to visit every record store in California, where he lives and works in the San Joaquin Valley. He is married and has two children. *Steven Sparrow & the Shade of a Great Tree* is his debut novel.

For more, visit:
www.matthewdalejones.com

www.ingramcontent.com/pod-product-compliance
Lightning Source LLC
Chambersburg PA
CBHW051226210726
48290CB00003B/819